WINGATE RUSHED SLOCUM

Slocum had one shot left. He aimed directly at Wingate's head. Wingate drove his knife at Slocum's leg.

Slocum involuntarily jerked away—and his shot missed Wingate's head. He yelled in rage and pain when the blade cut his thigh. Worse than the wound was the knowledge that his gun was empty.

He whipped out his own knife.

Wingate said. "You got guts, boy. And I'm gonna spread 'em all over the forest!"

OTHER BOOKS BY JAKE LOGAN

JAKE LOGAN

SLOCUM AND THE PREACHER'S DAUGHTER

BERKLEY BOOKS, NEW YORK

SLOCUM AND THE PREACHER'S DAUGHTER

A Berkley Book / published by arrangement with
the author

PRINTING HISTORY
Berkley edition / November 1988

ISBN: 0-425-11194-6

A BERKLEY BOOK ® TM 757,375
Berkley Books are published by The Berkley Publishing Group
200 Madison Avenue, New York, N.Y. 10016.
The name "BERKLEY" and the "B" logo
are trademarks belonging to Berkley Publishing Corporation.

PRINTED IN THE UNITED STATES OF AMERICA.

10 9 8 7 6 5 4 3 2 1

1

John Slocum stretched in the saddle, stood in his stirrups, and stared across the flat Oklahoma landscape. Spring 1881 had been kind to the territory after a harsh winter. New green showed through winter-burned grass, and the soft breeze made him feel glad to be alive. His sorrel shifted uneasily from hoof to hoof as she strained to reach a bit of the verdant grass.

"Take it easy, old girl," he said, patting her neck. "I don't rightly know where we're going, but we're not there yet." Two weeks on a Mississippi riverboat had proven fruitful for him. Five twenty-dollar gold pieces rode easily in his vest pocket. Slocum always enjoyed finding green-horns who didn't understand odds. Two of them had provided him with the double eagles and this fine horse over at Fort Smith, Arkansas.

He sucked in another lungful of the clean air laced with the sharp scent of plants growing frantically to reach the pale, warm spring sun. It felt good to be alive today. It felt damned good.

Slocum dismounted and let his sorrel nibble at the juicy grass as he walked around to stretch his aching joints. The time spent on the riverboat had turned him into a city slicker. He had gotten used to soft beds and three squares.

He didn't miss it a bit, though. The feel of a horse moving smoothly under him and the rain and wind in his face told him where he belonged. Slocum had no good idea where he was headed, nor did it much matter. When he didn't have anyone putting demands on him, he was as happy and free as a bird in flight.

Slocum stopped and cocked his head to one side. A faint rattling noise carried on the wind. Turning slowly, he homed in on the source. A series of low hills separated him from considerable clanking of chains, straining of leather harness, and general noise from overworked draft animals. Slocum's curiosity spurred him to get back in the saddle and stand in the stirrups once more to see the wellspring of all this commotion. In a few minutes the lead rig of the wagon train hove into view. Two oxen strained to pull the dragging Conestoga. A man dressed like a sodbuster with a blue bandanna wrapped around his neck cursed and shouted at the balky oxen.

Slocum watched with a wry smile. He had seen too many wagon trains like this. The settlers had gotten the bee into their bonnets that somewhere else was better farming, better weather, better land, better something—and just pulled up stakes and left home and hearth. As the wagon train made its slow progress around the hill and down the small valley stretching toward the north and west, the smile left his lips as memories returned to haunt him.

They just wanted something better from life for their wives and children. Slocum had had a taste of that after the war. He had returned a wounded man, barely able to walk. Slow months had put him right, but the ache caused by the deaths of his parents and his brother Robert gnawed at him something fierce.

The farm in Calhoun County, Georgia, had kept him busy and his mind from dwelling too much on all he had lost. It had been his bad luck that a carpetbagger judge had taken a fancy to the farm. Back taxes were owed, the crooked judge had said. Slocum had seen right off that no amount of money would save the farm. When the carpet-bagger and his hired gunman had ridden in one afternoon, only John Slocum had ridden out that night—leaving behind two fresh graves on the ridge by the spring house.

"Judge murderer" had been the way the wanted posters read. Slocum didn't even dignify what he had done as murder. It had been vermin killing. Still, the law didn't see it that way. Slocum had spent a considerable part of his life dodging lawmen intent on collecting a reward for that act so many years ago.

Slocum didn't blame the settlers for wanting to move on to better themselves. He had no idea what they were running from. He hoped none had the burden to carry that he did and that Oklahoma Territory would be the bonanza they sought.

He started to tug at the sorrel's reins and ride due west when a wagon train scout took off his broad-brimmed hat and waved at him from a distant ridge. He was too far away to see the man or hear what he shouted, but he recognized the battered hat instantly. Only one man sported such gaudy silver and gold conches with turquoise settings as a hatband.

Slocum laughed ruefully. Jethro August was about the last man in the world he expected to see in this neck of the woods. Slocum put his heels to the sorrel's sides and trotted forward.

August met him halfway to the wagon train's lead rig. "Slocum, you old son of a diseased gila monster!" The man rode closer and clapped Slocum on the shoulder so hard it rattled his teeth.

"You surely haven't changed, Jethro," Slocum allowed. "You still have terrible taste in hats, and you smell like a saloon."

"Haven't had a drink in weeks," the man said, looking pained at the notion that he drank. "'Cept maybe a nip or two to keep me warm at nights. Gets cold out on the trail."

"What are you doing herding these sodbusters?" Slocum asked. "Riding range is more your line of work."

August shook his head sadly, as if he had come to the end of a long and prosperous career. The bright spring sunlight caught the flashy hatband and sent rays of brilliance arrowing in all directions. Slocum squinted as he looked at his old friend. They hadn't seen one another since riding fence down in Texas for a medium-sized spread, well nigh four years back. Those had been good times for both of them.

"I had a passel of mighty bad luck, John. You can appreciate that."

"Law trouble?"

"They just don't understand how it is when I get a snootful of whiskey," Jethro said. "I *told* them to stand back and let me have my head. Damned fools didn't do it."

"Who got killed?"

"Nobody important," Jethro said, his mood brightening. "Damned certain it wasn't nobody who didn't deserve what he got." He held out his huge, gnarled hands and flexed them. "They tell me I strangled him. The man looked like a bull. No neck to speak of. Reckon it was something to see, but I don't remember much about it."

"They still looking for you?"

"Only Texas Rangers, and what do they care for anyone outside their territory? Might find myself in ass-deep trouble if I drifted south again, but I won't. I actually kind of like playing nursemaid for these greenhorns."

"You look to be doing it all by yourself. You haven't turned so cheap that you won't even hire a scout or an outrider to take some of the load off you?"

Slocum watched the man's face harden.

Jethro August shook his head and wiped sweat from his forehead. "You know how it can be, John. Damned near impossible at times keeping good help. I hired on three men back in Arkansas, where we formed the party. They're still back there a piece." Jethro pointed toward the Mississippi.

"Law trouble?"

"Damned fools," grumbled Jethro. "Can you believe it? They was doing their work all nice and fine for me, then taking time off to rob banks along the route. Even a dumb hick sheriff can figure out what's happening. They didn't seem to remember there are telegraph stations damned near everywhere, and anyone can send a wire."

"You're keeping them together alone?" Slocum indicated the long line of wagons struggling along. The going was easy here. Many of the prairie schooners needed repairs, and others lacked decent draft animals to pull wagons that had been too heavily laden. It got hard when men and women had to choose what to leave behind and what to take. Too often they tried to keep all their worldly possessions with them and thereby lost everything.

A good wagonmaster would have ordered the wagons lightened. Jethro August was a decent man, and his heart wasn't in telling people to leave their memories behind.

"John," he started. Slocum knew what was coming before Jethro spoke the words. "I need help. There's too damned many of them for me to ride herd on constantly. You wouldn't believe the fool things they get into, either. Without Dantley and the two yahoos that rode with him, I've been working twenty-hour days and getting damned little to eat and nothing in the way of sleep."

Slocum chuckled. Jethro August always exaggerated. From the size of the paunch hanging over his gunbelt, he hadn't missed too many meals in the past month.

"This isn't my kind of work," Slocum said. The expression on Jethro's face made him reconsider. "You're asking me as a friend, aren't you?" he asked.

"John, this is important. I only got another couple weeks to spend with these fine people before they arrive. Maybe less. Oklahoma's got some land grants opening. The government's been talking about doing it for years, and one day soon they'll open up damned near all the territory, mark my words. I got a nice bonus riding on them getting there for the first day."

"Stealing land from the Indians," muttered Slocum.

"Not like that. Not this time. This is land just outside the Cherokee Nation up by Broken Arrow and was hardly claimed by them. Well, not much, at any rate. It's real important for the sodbusters to be ready when the land office opens. They're getting some prime farmland to build their sod houses on."

Slocum had no place to go and simply drifted, but he had money in his pocket and no desire to look after a wagon train filled with farmers and their families.

"I'll give you a hundred dollars in scrip or eighty in gold for two weeks' work, John. It's that important to me."

"Eighty dollars?" Slocum said, startled at Jethro's generosity. Not for an instant did he consider the hundred dollars in greenbacks. They were mostly worthless as far as he was concerned, except for starting campfires.

"It'll be the easiest money you ever made, John. And you'll be doing an old friend a big favor. I *need* the help. I'm swaying in my saddle from being on poor old Paint's back too long."

Slocum studied the mangy creature Jethro rode. It looked to be the same horse he had owned down in Texas. If anything, it had become even more swaybacked under the load it carried.

"The only time I get into trouble is helping out friends," Slocum said.

"I can't rightly say you owe me, John. If anything, it's the other way around. I remember when you got me out of that den of thieves down in Nuevo Laredo. I thought I was a goner for sure that night. How many was it? Eight of them varmints what attacked me?"

"It was only two," Slocum said, smiling as he remembered the bar fight. Two vaqueros hadn't taken kindly to remarks Jethro had made about their *patrón*. The fight had been a knock-down-drag-out. Slocum had done his share of knocking down, but he had also dragged Jethro out before the drunken man had been too badly hurt.

"I owe you, not the other way around," Jethro went on. "But I need this favor from you, John. I swear to Christ Almighty, I thought my heart was going to stop when I saw you sitting there all ready to move on."

"Two weeks?" Slocum asked. The grin spreading on Jethro August's face told that the wagonmaster knew he had hired him the best scout possible. Slocum owed him nothing, but the money sounded mighty good to him, even with more than that riding high and hard in his pocket.

"Might be less. I guarantee not a day longer than two

weeks, no matter what, John. You won't regret this. I promise. They're a good bunch, even if they don't know their ass from a hole in the ground when it comes to driving wagons."

"I saw," Slocum said, eyeing the third wagon in the train. Its rear axle creaked ominously and threatened to snap at any instant. "That one needs work to keep it rolling."

"That's old man Sneed. One hell of a blowhard, but he's a good worker when he puts his mind to it. Just tell him what he's got to do. You won't have to ride him too hard to see that he does it."

Jethro August reached over and slapped Slocum on the back again. "Thanks, John. You won't regret it. I promise."

"What do you want me to do?"

Jethro sobered quickly. "I been counting the wagons rolling by, and there's one missing. Can you backtrack for a few miles and see what's happened? Don't want any of them spending the night away from the rest of the wagon train."

"Sounds easy," Slocum said. He turned the sorrel along the train's path and started off. Jethro August yelled his thanks after him, then let out a whoop of joy and galloped off toward the front of the line of wagons.

Slocum rode slowly, his quick green eyes studying the path chewed up by the heavy wagon wheels. Two miles toward the Illinois River he found a single set of wagon tracks going straight north. He shook his head in dismay. The way the river curled around meant the driver would have to cross the Illinois a second time. Slocum wondered why the sodbuster hadn't stayed with the main wagon train.

There was no accounting for the way a tenderfoot thought.

Slocum picked up the pace when he heard a rifle shot. He couldn't believe the wagon had left the others simply to hunt. A second shot echoing down the narrow valley caused him to put his heels into the sorrel's side. Something was wrong. He felt it in his bones.

Topping a rise, he got a good look down the humidity-hazed valley. A smaller stream fed into the Illinois before it flowed into the Arkansas. Grass had turned lush from the spring runoff water and caused the banks to become treacherously slick and muddy. The sodbuster's wagon had slewed to one side and gotten two wheels stuck in the mud.

But that was the least of his problems.

More rifles shots sounded. Slocum saw two Choctaw braves dismount and slip through the underbrush near the stream's edge. The knives they carried showed their intent. They circled the luckless sodbuster, who fired wildly in the direction of three other braves.

Slocum heaved a deep sigh. Jethro August had said there wouldn't be any reason to regret signing on with the wagon train for two weeks. He hadn't been on the job two hours and he already faced possible death—and if he did nothing or simply rode off, the farmer would end up easy prey for the skilled Choctaw raiders.

Reaching forward, he pulled his Winchester from its saddle scabbard. He swung it around, cocked it smoothly, and brought it to his shoulder. One Choctaw heard the sound and spun. Slocum's shot caught him high on the right shoulder and sent him spinning into the stream. A second shot missed. A tiny fountain of water showed that he had overshot his target by almost a foot.

Slocum cursed. Shooting uphill was hard; he thought shooting downhill might be worse. He had been a sniper during the war, one of the best the South had. Missing by so much made him angry.

He took a long, deep, calming breath and fired again. This one sent the wounded Choctaw scuttling for cover. The other raider stared up the rise at Slocum, then looked over his shoulder at the sodbuster. The brave made a quick decision and attacked.

Slocum cursed even louder this time. The brave ran low through the brush, making himself into a difficult target. Slocum fired twice more and missed both times. With the farmer busy with the other Indians, he didn't even see the brave sneaking up on him.

Slocum yelled to get the man's attention. The roar from the man's ponderous Sharps drowned out any words of warning. The sorrel balked on its way down the steep slope and kept Slocum from getting in another shot. He regained control of his horse, but knew he would be too late. The man's throat would be slit by the time he reached the stream.

Slocum splashed loudly through the stream in the direction of the mired wagon. He saw the Choctaw rise up behind the hapless sodbuster, ready to kill.

A single sharp, distinct shot cut through the din. The Choctaw raider stiffened and spun to the side, as if starting a crazy dance. He slumped to the ground, dead.

"Get down, mister, get down!" Slocum shouted. He pulled his horse to a halt and jumped to the ground. Seeing that their easy victim had reinforcements, the other three braves melted into the thicket. A few minutes later Slocum heard the hollow pounding of unshod horses' hooves against the dry, packed earth.

"They're gone," he said, wiping sweat from his forehead. "Why did you leave the wagon train? That was a damnfool thing to do."

Slocum looked up when a pregnant woman emerged from the wagon bed. The sodbuster helped her down. He tried to speak, then stopped, gathered his wits, and made another try. "Me and the missus wasn't too sure if we could ford the Arkansas when Mr. August intended. We decided to look for an easier ford, what with her in this condition and all."

Slocum shook his head. "The others in the train would have helped you. That's why you travel together. A band of raiders off the reservation would never have attacked the wagon train like this."

"Mr. August kept telling us that there was strength in numbers," the woman said primly. "My husband is overly solicitous of my condition." She rested her hands on her distended belly.

"A widow woman and a child raised by Indians is a sight worse than getting bounced around crossing a river," said Slocum.

"You work for Mr. August?" the woman asked. She wasn't as shaken as her husband. Slocum knew who wore the britches in this family.

"Yes, ma'am. He sent me out to see what had become of you. I arrived in the nick of time, it seems."

Slocum walked around the wagon, studying how badly mired it was and trying to figure what had happened to the Choctaw trying to slit the sodbuster's throat.

"You didn't happen to have a pistol in there with you, did you?" Slocum asked.

"Don't be absurd, sir. Of course not. I'd never touch one of those things."

Slocum frowned. Who had killed the brave?

He turned at a sudden noise in the thicket and caught a glimpse of a smallish rider wearing a tan canvas duster and a bright red bandanna. Then the man vanished and left behind nothing but fading echoes.

Slocum scratched his head. He didn't see why anyone would save the farmer and his pregnant wife, then ride away without so much as a by-your-leave.

"Better get your wagon free of this mudbank and back to the train," he said. With his sorrel pulling and the sod-buster's two scrawny mules straining, they got the wagon out of the muck and rolling easily.

All the way back to the wagon train Slocum looked for some sign of the mysterious rifleman who had saved the farmer. Whoever he was, he rode like a ghost and didn't leave a trail.

2

"Is there any further danger, Mr. Slocum?" asked the woman from the wagon's high, hard seat.

"I doubt it," he said, his sharp green eyes roving constantly over the countryside. "The Indian raiders were looking for easy victims. Chasing them off turned them cautious, leastwise as far as we're concerned."

"Do you believe they'll get reinforcements and return?" the woman asked.

Slocum shook his head. Choctaws didn't fight that way. These were a few braves off the reservation to the south. They might have gotten liquored up and anxious to prove themselves. Slocum didn't reckon the handful of Indians were any real danger and told the settlers so.

"I find it difficult to believe that the lawmen allow such ruffians to go about molesting innocent people as they did," the woman said stiffly.

"Might I inquire where you're from, ma'am? Not from these parts."

"Sir, I am from Boston. My family came over on the Mayflower."

Slocum smiled as he rode ahead. Things in Oklahoma Territory were a mite different from Boston society, where it mattered how you or your people got to this country. Out here staying alive was a full-time concern. He almost asked why she had come so far from home but bit back the question. How did anyone find themselves settling west of the Mississippi?

Many sought, few found.

"Either of you have any idea who helped us out back there? I've been looking for some tracks and haven't found any."

"What are you saying?" the woman asked. *"You* chased off those brutal savages."

"There was another rifleman. He shot the Choctaw trying to cut your husband's throat. I caught a glimpse as he rode off, but all I saw was a red bandanna and a canvas duster."

"Can't say I know anyone answering to that description," the sodbuster said. "I'd be more'n happy to thank him, too. This is all something of a nightmare for us."

Slocum didn't reply. He was lost in thought as he fell into the easy rhythm of his walking horse. They rejoined the wagon train just before sundown. For this small miracle Slocum gave a silent prayer of thanks. He had no desire to be out on the trail with two greenhorns and a wagon that needed some fixing. He had checked the wheels after getting it pried free of the mire and found the bearings sorely in need of greasing. It wasn't anything needing immediate attention, but the wheels would lock up if they didn't get some lubrication within a few hours. The mud had seeped into everything.

Jethro August came riding up, a worried look on his face. "You all right, Mrs. Throckmorton? You surely did give me a fright going off by yourself like that."

Slocum noticed that his friend ignored the man and spoke directly to the head of the family.

"Mr. Slocum served us admirably. He is worlds better than those rowdies hired originally. What were their names?"

"Dantley, Brighton, and a Mexican fellow named Villalobos." Jethro didn't look any too happy remembering the trio.

"They were scoundrels, sir, and we told you that from day one. They weren't gentlemen like Mr. Slocum."

Slocum tipped his hat and grinned. He wondered how Mrs. Throckmorton would react if she knew he had killed a judge back in Calhoun County, Georgia. Not well, he suspected.

"We've made good time today, John," Jethro told him when they were out of earshot of the Throckmortons. "We'd've done better if it hadn't been for them and their damnfool maneuvering away from the wagon train."

"He's worried about his wife. Can't fault a man for that," Slocum said. As they walked beside the wagons, he studied each one for the man who had rescued Throckmorton from the Indian's knife. "Who else besides us left the train today? It'd be a man on horseback."

"No one that I know about," Jethro said. "I discourage them from wandering off by themselves. With the way they act, they'd be in the middle of trouble within an hour."

"This gent can handle himself," said Slocum. He told his friend about the mysterious rider.

"We owe him a debt of gratitude. He saved me purt near fifty dollars. If'n I'd lost the Throckmortons I'd've lost their 'timely arrival' bonus."

"That much? No wonder you can afford to be so generous."

"Don't go getting any ideas, John. Not everyone's paying so handsomely. And expenses are higher than a buckin' bronc's back, too. I got fees, I got—"

"Never mind." Slocum waved the protest aside. "I believe you. There's not going to be a repeat of today's muddle. No one's getting away without my knowing it."

"Good thing, too, what with the Indians on the warpath and all," Jethro said.

Slocum shook his head. "Those were just renegades off the reservation who got to whooping it up. They weren't a serious war party. They wouldn't have run so quick if they had been."

"Still, keep an eye peeled for them. I don't want any more delays. Two weeks, John. That's all I got to get them to Broken Arrow and the damned land office."

"You worry too much for your own good, Jethro."

"You're right. You always were. What do you say to a small nip of red-eye to celebrate you signing on?"

"Later. I want to check on everyone to be sure they've bedded down for the night."

"I hired you to look after them, not be a mother hen," Jethro said gruffly. Slocum heard the tone of approval in the wagonmaster's voice, though.

He walked slowly the length of the wagon train, greeting people and introducing himself. Slocum would just as soon have ignored the people, and he would have except for his curiosity. He wanted to find the man who had saved the sodbuster's scalp that afternoon. There wasn't any good reason for the man to hide his identity.

One wagon had been pulled slightly away from the others. Slocum went to investigate when he heard someone speaking in a low, intense voice.

"I say unto you, beware of the Devil! Satan walks among us. He is everywhere—and he is working his way into your heart. Yes, I say, into *your* heart!"

Slocum stopped and stared. A short man dressed in a long black swallowtail coat stood on a box pulled close to a tiny cooking fire. The night breeze pulled sluggishly at the tails and made the man appear to have abnormally thick legs.

Dancing shadows from the fire turned the preacher man into something as satanic as the devil he warned against. He had high cheekbones and a thick, long nose—a Roman nose, Slocum had heard it called. The puffy lips, along with the ever-shifting shadows, gave him a cruel look. Slocum had seen worse in his day, but he wouldn't want to cross this man if he got in a rage.

"Brother, what can I do for you?" the preacher asked, hand resting on a leather-bound Bible.

"Just hired on today," Slocum explained. "I wondered why your wagon was pulled away from the others. We almost lost the Throckmortons this afternoon when they . . . got lost." Slocum didn't like pointing out others' stupidity, even when they deserved it. The sodbuster and his wife seemed harmless enough, even if they didn't belong out on the prairie.

"I do not like to disturb the rest of those in the wagon train when I practice my sermons."

"That's downright thoughtful of you," Slocum said.

"Is that disdain in your voice, sir?"

"No insult intended, preacher. Seems to me you'd want the others to hear you."

"I do, on Sundays. Forcing myself on them before then

takes away some of the impact of my words."

Slocum had never considered that preachers had to practice their hellfire-and-brimstone delivery. He'd thought it just rolled out naturally. "Didn't mean to disturb you at your work," he said.

"Please, forgive me," the minister said. "When I'm interrupted, I lose my manners. My name is Cole Mason." He thrust out a strong hand for Slocum to shake.

As Slocum moved closer, he had the feeling he had seen the man before. "Do I know you?" he asked. "You're face is distinctive, but—"

"I don't think we've met before," Mason said hurriedly. Too hurriedly for Slocum's liking. It made him think the short, stocky man was hiding something.

"Papa, do you know where . . ." The lilting, almost musical voice stopped abruptly. Slocum turned to see a tallish young woman standing beside the preacher's wagon, a tin can in her hands.

If Slocum thought he'd met Cole Mason before, he certainly wished he had met this dark-haired beauty long ago. She stood firmly erect, her shoulders back and her breasts straining against the front of her dark gingham dress. Bold blue eyes stared at him in a way he had to consider challenging. She and her father were about the same height, and from the fire Slocum saw in both, the physical was only one way they were similar.

"Who are you?" she asked bluntly.

"Dear, this is Mr. Slocum. Mr. August hired him today to take the place of the others we lost."

"The bank robbers?" she said. The young woman stepped closer. Slocum got a better look at her—and appreciated her beauty all the more. She had inherited her father's cheekbones, but the nose was smaller, more petite, far more feminine. He guessed this was a contribution on her mother's part. She lacked her father's harshness of feature.

The more he saw of her the more he liked.

"Evening, Miss Mason," he said. He introduced himself to her. She held out a long-fingered hand. He expected her to shake hands by dangling her fingers in his grip like most women. She surprised him with the firmness of her grip. She shook hands like a man—and she didn't seem too inclined to let go of his hand when they were done.

"I'm Grace Mason. Papa always forgets his manners when he's working on a new sermon. Did you hear it?"

"Part of it, Miss Mason. It sounded good. Inspiring." He wondered what her father would think if he were bold enough to call her by her first name. Slocum decided not to press his luck.

Besides, thin tendrils of memory kept floating by, just out of reach, telling him he had met Cole Mason before. And Mason hadn't been a preacher man then.

"I couldn't find the knife to open this can of peaches," Grace said to her father, holding the tin can out at arm's length.

"I was using it earlier. What did I do with it?" Mason wondered aloud.

"That's all right. Allow me." Slocum reached behind his back to the thick-bladed knife he kept sheathed there. He pulled it out and used it to cut away the lid.

"Would you join us in dinner, Mr. Slocum?" the dark-haired woman asked.

He started to say no but hesitated long enough for the preacher to second his daughter's suggestion.

"We have enough to share," Mason said.

"If Mrs. Mason doesn't mind," Slocum said, looking around.

"My wife is dead," the preacher said solemnly. "No,

don't apologize. How could you have known? She passed beyond this vale of tears almost six years ago, when Grace was fourteen. It has been a trial raising her, but I've done what I could."

"You've got a daughter any man could be proud of," Slocum said, his green eyes locking with Grace's brilliant blue ones.

"Thank you."

"Please, Mr. Slocum, sit here beside me." Grace Mason patted a spot on a log next to her.

Slocum didn't have to be asked twice, but he felt the preacher's hot eyes on him as he ate. The meal was simple, but it had been a long day and he had eaten only a few slices of fried salt pork for breakfast. The canned peaches slid down his throat and made him think life truly was worth living. "That's just what I needed," he said. "Thank you both very much for the victuals."

"Is that all you need, Mr. Slocum?" Grace asked.

Slocum wasn't sure if her father had overheard the tone she used. It said more than the simple words. "Got rounds to make, Miss Mason."

"Come back and see . . . us," she said.

Slocum smiled broadly, wondering how a preacher's daughter had grown up so bold. The smile faded as he walked along, thinking hard. Where *had* he seen Cole Mason before?

He was interrupted by Jethro August. "John, come quick. We got big trouble brewing down at the south end of camp. This is more'n I can handle by my lonesome."

"What is it?"

"A bounty hunter's come makin' trouble for us. Come along, hurry, damn you."

Slocum reached over and pulled the leather thong off the hammer of his Colt Navy. The ebony-handled pistol slid easily up and down in the soft leather holster as he strode along beside Jethro August.

"He came roarin' into camp screamin' about finding some damned bank robber. I told him Dantley and the others were already in jail, but he didn't want none of that. He said he's lookin' for someone else."

"Who?"

The answering roar made Slocum spin, hand flashing to the butt of his pistol.

"I'm Pisser Wingate and I come here to take back into custody one William Edward Deutsch, wanted in St. Louis for bank robbing and other sordid crimes."

Slocum stared at the mountain of a man and wondered if a Sharps .69 would bring him down. A Colt Navy—or any six-shooter—hardly seemed adequate for the job. Wingate stood six foot six and towered over Slocum. Of the three hundred pounds he carried, Wingate showed no hint of flab. His long hair had been greased down with lard that had turned rancid weeks ago, and his leather-fringe buckskins had become black from wear. Slocum couldn't tell if the man ever took them off. From the odor, he doubted it.

"Where the fuck is he?" roared Wingate. "The son of a bitch is around here somewhere. I can smell a criminal like him a mile off."

"You couldn't smell a skunk if you stepped on it," Slocum said. His nose twitched as Pisser Wingate stormed past.

"What's that, boy? What did you say?" Wingate's breath matched the power of his body odor.

"We don't know any William Deutsch," Slocum said, not sure if Jethro did or not. "You a bounty hunter?"

"What do I look like, boy? I ain't the Easter bunny." Wingate's immense hams of hands opened and closed, as if he felt the neck bones of his victim snapping. Jethro August was large; Wingate was immense.

And Slocum found that the bounty hunter moved with lightning speed. He had twitched slightly—and Wingate's powerful hand flashed out and closed on his wrist.

"Don't go annoying me, boy. I'll chew you up and spit you out." He grunted as he levered Slocum up onto his toes and heaved. Slocum kept his balance but had to struggle to do so. In a test of strength, few men could match Pisser Wingate.

Slocum vowed never to try. Wingate was the type of man you shot from ambush—using a large-caliber rifle.

"There's no one on this wagon train named Deutsch," said Jethro. "And I don't want you bothering any of the good people here, either. They put in a hard day on the trail and deserve to rest." Jethro August took a step back from the bounty hunter when the wind shifted.

"I don't give a diddly shit what they want. I followed him halfway across the country, and I'm taking him back to St. Lou, dead or alive."

"Let's see your warrant," said Slocum. He moved to keep Wingate between him and Jethro. Should the man attack either of them, the other had Wingate's broad back for a target.

"Don't need none. I *know* the toad's around here. I tell you, boy, I can *smell* him."

"No warrant, no search," said Slocum.

"I got no time to talk with you, boy." Wingate swung around and started for the wagons. Jethro moved to stop him, but the bounty hunter struck him hard on the side of the head. August was a huge man, but he went sailing like a feather caught on a tornado.

Slocum didn't hesitate. He dropped to his side and kicked out. His foot drove fast between Wingate's ankles, causing the man to topple like a felled tree. Wingate landed hard, and the air wheezed out of his lungs.

Before Slocum could get to his feet Jethro had gotten to his, drawn his pistol, and stuck it behind the bounty hunter's ear. Slocum saw Jethro's hand tremble as he struggled with the moral dilemma of whether to kill Pisser Wingate.

"He's not worth a murder charge up here, too, Jethro," he said softly.

"Damn it, you're right, John. Truss him up good and proper, drag him out—and don't worry none if the rope gets tangled up around his neck. I want him away from the wagon train." Jethro looked around to see if the ruckus had drawn any attention. It hadn't.

Like a striking snake, Jethro swung the barrel of his six-shooter up and down, landing it on the top of Wingate's head. The crunch echoed through the still night air. Without another word Jethro stalked off.

Slocum bound the bounty hunter hand and foot, then struggled to get him up and over his saddle. He considered dragging him from the camp as Jethro had suggested but decided against it. Pisser Wingate wasn't the kind to take a hint, but Slocum didn't want to be the cause of his death any more than he'd wanted Jethro to pull the trigger.

He looked around before he rode out with the bounty hunter to make sure no one in the camp had been disturbed. Slocum's sharp eyes caught only a small movement in the thicket.

One person had seen his fight with Wingate: Grace Mason.

He felt her brilliant blue eyes on him as he left with the bounty hunter.

3

Pisser Wingate struggled and thrashed about, but Slocum had bound him too well for the enormous bounty hunter to escape. Slocum put a double loop of rope around the huge man's ankles and then tossed the free end over a sturdy cottonwood limb. A bit of urging got Wingate's horse to hoist the man up so he dangled head down. As he fought his bonds, he turned slowly. Slocum saw hatred burning in the man's piglike red eyes.

If he hadn't gagged him, Slocum knew what the bounty hunter would have been saying. He still tried shouting through the rag stuffed in his mouth.

"I've smeared a tad of honey on the ropes," Slocum said. "Ants ought to chew through in a day or two, if you're lucky." Slocum's words turned winter-cold. "If you've got any brains in that thick skull, you'll hightail it in the opposite direction and not show your ugly face around the wagon train again."

Wingate's muffled protests faded in the distance as Slocum rode away. He had the feeling they hadn't seen the last of Pisser Wingate. Throughout the West there were men who simply didn't fit into polite society. Wingate was obviously one of them. Even for a mountain man, he smelled bad. Slocum rubbed his running nose. The smell from the lard Wingate used on his hair had made it drip.

The clear night air washed away any lingering odor and settled about Slocum like a fine blanket. Stars shone above brilliantly, and the white band of stars arching from southwest to northeast gave enough light to see the trail without straining. Times like this made Slocum feel as if he could whip his weight in wildcats.

He rode back into camp. Most of the cooking fires had died to embers, and the sodbusters had gone to sleep. Slocum made a slow circuit of the camp and found Jethro August sitting with his back against a tree, a bottle in a trembly hand.

"Get rid of that son of a bitch, John?"

"He won't be bothering us anytime soon," Slocum said, not really believing it. He wondered if he should have taken to heart Jethro's order to hang Wingate. The bounty hunter wasn't the kind of man to give up easily, especially not when he had been humiliated.

"Good. Son of a bitch can't come dancin' into *my* camp and raise hell. No siree bob. Can't." Jethro turned a bleary eye toward Slocum. "Want a little pull on my medicine?" He held the bottle out.

Slocum dismounted and tethered his horse. He sank down beside his friend and took the whiskey bottle. Fire raced down his gullet as he took a healthy swig of the liquor. "Where in hell did you get this?" he asked breathlessly. The potent liquor refused to stop burning in his belly.

"Bottled hellfire, they called it. Got it from some gents back in Arkansas. Good, ain't it?"

"Never tasted anything like it," Slocum said.

Jethro August heaved a sigh and stared through the tree branches at the stars. "Can't think of a place I'd rather be than out here. So peaceful. Nobody yammering at you."

"You've got a wagon train full of greenhorns all demanding you help them," Slocum pointed out. He took another drag on the bottle, this time tempering his thirst with memory of the first drink. It still burned throat and gut.

"They quiet down till around dawn," Jethro told him. "They aren't so bad. Just damned fools who don't know what they're doing or where they're going—only they want to get there quick-like."

Silence fell between the men as they drank, Slocum more slowly than Jethro. When the bottle came up empty, Jethro said, "'Bout time for me to make some rounds and see that they're all bedded down proper." He tried to stand and fell back to the ground.

"You rest up for tomorrow," Slocum said. "I'll see to them. I've got to find a place to bed down anyway."

"Thank you, John. You're a decent man, no matter what they say about you." Jethro August's head dropped, his chin resting on his chest. In seconds he snored loudly.

Slocum laughed as he led his horse through the center of the wagon train's encampment. Few stirred at this late hour, and no one had seen the unpleasant row with the bounty hunter.

No one except Grace Mason.

Slocum's steps turned toward the preacher's wagon. The cook fire had died, and not even embers remained. He wondered how the man kept warm as he slept a few feet away, a thin blanket pulled tightly around his shoulders.

Even though it was a fine Oklahoma spring, the night had turned cold.

"Hellfire and brimstone," came a soft voice from the shadows beyond the wagon.

Slocum's hand flashed to the butt of his Colt Navy. Even as he felt the cold pistol under his fingers, he relaxed. He recognized the velvety voice.

"How's that?" he asked Grace Mason.

"You were wondering how my father stays warm without a fire at night. His dreams of hellfire and damnation are more than adequate for the task." A tinge of bitterness crept into her voice when she spoke of her father.

"You don't approve?"

"Of course I do. He does God's work, doesn't he? Sin is everywhere, and he roots it out with a diligence that is sometimes frightening in its intensity."

Slocum let the issue die.

Grace walked noiselessly and stopped beside him. She might have been a ghost in the night. The starlight turned her face into a pale oval and her hair into raven cascades with silver highlights. Slocum might have seen a more beautiful woman, but he couldn't rightly remember when.

"Why aren't you asleep? The wagon train's got a hard day's travel ahead. You need all the rest you can get."

"I was . . . restless," she said, taking his arm. "Come walk with me. Just tether your horse here. No one's going to steal him."

"Her," Slocum corrected automatically.

"That's a start," she said cryptically.

"Toward what?" he asked.

"You know the difference between male and female." Before he could reply, she changed the subject on him, saying, "What was it that awful man wanted tonight?"

"It was nothing. He got lost and I had to put him back on the right trail."

"You have interesting ways of direction, Mr. Slocum. I do believe you dragged him out of camp with a rope tied around his ankles. His horse had to strain to carry him as fast as you wanted to ride."

"The horse was probably tuckered out from a hard day's travel."

"There you go again, talking about sleep. Is that *all* you can think of?"

"I'm going to be doing some hard work tomorrow, Miss Mason—"

"Call me Grace and I'll call you John."

"Fair enough, if you don't think your father would mind or consider it the work of the Devil."

"He would," she said, startling him. "Papa thinks *everything* is the work of Satan. He just doesn't know how to have any fun."

Something in the woman's words caused Slocum to tense. What was her idea of fun? He wasn't quite sure.

"There. See it?" she asked. "The shooting star. They're supposed to be good luck. You can make a wish on it."

"Grace . . ."

"Hurry, John. Make a wish." She closed her bright blue eyes and turned her face toward the sky. He looked down at her and couldn't resist the temptation. She was more than beautiful. She was beguiling and gorgeous.

He kissed her full on the lips.

She responded instantly, her arms going around his neck and pulling him down hard. The kiss deepened and took Slocum's breath away. They finally broke apart, both gasping.

"It works," Grace said. "I made a wish and got it right away."

Slocum knew better than to get involved with the daughter of a preacher and one of the men he was supposed to be leading. Such affairs always carried considerable risk.

But Grace Mason was too pretty to resist, and she had been a willing ally.

She grabbed his hand and pulled him along, deeper into the scrubby wooded area and away from the camp. He knew better, but he followed anyway.

"I've been exploring. That's when I saw you with that horrible man. What was his name again?"

"Don't remember saying," Slocum said. "What's your interest in him?"

"Bounty hunters fascinate me," she said. "He *was* a bounty hunter, wasn't he?"

"He got off on the wrong trail. I put him right. He won't be coming back to annoy us again."

"I saw how you handled him. He looked like a grizzly bear, and you had no trouble at all with him. You're so strong and brave, John."

He had heard come-ons like this a dozen times from saloon whores. Somehow, the words coming from Grace sounded different. He knew them for what they were, but they excited him, made him feel good. She had that way about her.

They stood in a small, grassy clearing, a circle of sky open above them. Another shooting star hurtled across the heavens and exploded with a brilliant green flash.

"A fireball. They're rare," Grace said. "That requires a special wish."

He reached out and touched her cheek. She closed her eyes and rocked her head to one side, trapping his hand between cheek and shoulder. She moved closer. The wind caught a hint of her perfume and brought it to his nostrils. It excited him even more.

They kissed again. She pressed close to him, her lush body rubbing constantly and arousing him. By the time her fingers worked down the front of his shirt, unbuttoning it, he knew there was no turning back, even if he'd wanted to.

He cast aside his gunbelt and ran his hands through her dark, silky hair. She tipped her head back again for another kiss. Her lips gleamed wetly in the starlight. The kiss set his pulse racing hard.

But he thought he would explode when she unbuttoned his trousers and thrust her hand down inside.

"What's this?" she whispered as she nibbled at his ear. "It's long and hard and hot." She squeezed. He almost lost control.

"Careful," he said. "It's been a while for me."

"I doubt that. A man like you can have any woman he wants."

He stared at her through the night and saw the wide grin on her face. He pulled her closer, kissing her hard. Their passions ignited. Somehow, they worked on each other's clothing and finally got it off. The cold night wind caused a ripple of gooseflesh to pass along Slocum's backside, but the warmth at his groin let him ignore it.

He stared down at the woman under him. She might have been a demon sent to tempt him—or she might have been an angel.

"Does your pa approve of you going off in the woods with the hired help?" he asked.

"Papa approves of nothing," she said, sighing deeply. "He has no idea how to enjoy himself."

She showed Slocum she had some interesting ideas on how to enjoy herself. Grace's fingers ran down his sides, teasing and tickling until the flesh burned. When she found his manhood again and tightened her fingers around it, he gasped.

"What's this?" she asked. "Why, I do declare, I do believe you have a hard-on." She giggled and tugged at him.

Slocum sank down on top of her body, feeling her breasts crush between them. He decided it was his turn to torment her a little. One hand reached underneath and grabbed a fleshy buttock. The other roamed across her chest, teasing first one and then the other rosy nipple. When his lips closed on the left one, Grace gasped.

"More," she sobbed out. "Don't stop now. I need more. I need you so much, John. More!"

He wasn't about to stop when paradise beckoned. He tongued her nipples and left trails of saliva on her breasts that gleamed silver and bright in the starlight.

Lifting her buttock with one hand, he opened willing thighs with the other. Sliding between her legs, he thought he would soon be inside her.

He was wrong. Like a greased pig, she squealed and twisted, getting out from under him in a flash. She rolled on the ground and came to her feet a few paces away.

"It's not going to be that easy, John. You've got to catch me."

"Grace, we're buck naked. We can't go running around in the woods. Someone from the wagon train might see us."

"I know!" With that, the sleek young woman ran across the grassy clearing, stopping in the middle and beckoning to him. "Catch me, John. You've got to catch me if you want me!"

"Grace!" He saw that appealing to her wouldn't do any good. He got to his feet and ran after her. She laughed in delight and ran for the far side of the clearing—but he caught her easily after a minute's chase.

He swung her around and kissed her again. Her cheeks were flushed and her breasts heaved in a way he found completely captivating. But as they parted, she wiggled like a fish and got away from him again.

It took several quick steps for him to circle her waist with his arms and lift her off her feet.

"Got you this time!" he cried.

When he put her back down, Grace came to rest on the ground on hands and knees, the round, fleshy curve of her rear too enticing to resist. He dropped down behind her, waiting for her to protest. When she didn't, Slocum edged forward on his knees. His hardness parted the white moons of her rump and ran along the moist crevice he found there.

He gasped when she reached back between her legs and caught at him, guiding him, positioning him just right.

"Now, John. There's where I want it. Please." This time she begged rather than ran. His hips moved forward, and he sank into her dampness. Grace gasped as he rushed into her, and powerful muscles clamped down all around him. Slocum fought to keep from spilling his seed. He wanted to enjoy this sensation for as long as he could.

He bent over her, chest against her back. His hands found her breasts. As if milking a cow, he began pulling at them. Grace gasped and began to shake all over like a leaf in a high wind.

"I love what you do to me, John. More, do it more!"

His hands stroked her breasts, moved along her heaving belly, found the insides of her thighs. All the while his hands roamed, his hips moved back and forth with deliberate strokes.

Being buried inside her was heaven. When he pulled free, a cool wind whipping across the meadow turned him to ice. It was better to be in the woman's clutching hot cavity than to be outside.

His arm circled her waist and lifted. Her firm buttocks fitted perfectly into the curve of his groin. Harder and faster he sought to sink into her. Grace began shoving her hips back to meet his every thrust. Together they thrashed and ground and strove.

She gasped and then cried out in the night. For an instant he worried about someone coming to investigate and finding them locked together like two dogs. Then a fever tide rose within him and drowned any such thoughts. His balls burned as they contracted. His cock ached with need. Slocum moved faster and faster, friction taking its toll on his control.

He exploded in her tightness like a stick of dynamite going off.

Sagging forward, he still held her close. They lay on their sides like two spoons in a drawer.

"What are you thinking, John?" she asked.

He grinned. "Wishing on a falling star seems to work. And it's even better when you wish on a fireball."

They laughed, and then Grace Mason proved again that wishes come true when they saw another falling star. It was almost dawn before Slocum returned to the wagon train, tired but happier than he had been in months.

4

Slocum ached from his amorous activities with Grace Mason three nights prior. Every time the sorrel moved under him new waves of agony jolted through him. It had been too long since he'd found a woman with the fire shown by the preacher's daughter. He yawned widely, then settled down and ignored any discomfort. He didn't regret an instant of the time he'd spent with Grace.

While the wagons got repaired and the animals rested, Jethro August had sent him ahead of the train to find fords to be used over the next few days. The Illinois and Canadian rivers merged and went gushing on through to the Arkansas. Spring runoff swelled the rivers and made travel for the heavy wagons hazardous. In spite of this, Slocum saw little problem getting the wagon train across the Illinois and would tell the wagonmaster this when he returned. But today he had duties that reached beyond the train.

Fort Gibson lay only a half day's ride for him, and he

didn't hesitate taking a detour to reach it. The town had been around since 1824 and had played an important role in the war. Slocum's interest didn't lie there but in a nagging memory.

He had seen Cole Mason before and couldn't remember where. He hoped that the trip to Fort Gibson would prod his memory. The preacher and his daughter had come up from Arkansas to settle, but Slocum followed a gut-level instinct that he could find something around the fort or the town that would spur his memory.

He reined in when he came to the main road leading into Fort Gibson. Cavalry troopers walked along the hard-packed dirt street, their brass buttons shining in the bright afternoon sun. He watched them cautiously. Even after all these years, he had never taken to liking Yankee soldiers. He had killed too many during the war—and they had killed his brother Robert.

For John Slocum some memories died hard.

"Mister, got a light?" called a trooper lounging in front of Zeke Parson's General Store. The man held up a quirly.

"Reckon I do," said Slocum, dismounting. Swallowing his distaste for soldiers might allow him to get needed information quickly. He fumbled in his pocket and found a lucifer. He struck it and held it out for the soldier, who puffed furiously for a few seconds to produce a blue smoke cloud, then leaned back and stared at Slocum.

"You a smokin' man? I can offer you one of these. They're not too good, but it's yours for the price of the lucifer you were so generous with." The soldier patted his pocket. Slocum saw several more quirlies poking out.

"Haven't had a good smoke in a month of Sundays," Slocum allowed, thinking that these weren't likely to be good smokes, either. The trooper passed one over. Slocum used a second lucifer to light it and inhaled. The smoke filled his lungs and sent a shiver of pleasure through his body. The bent and twisted quirly tasted better than it had any right to. "Best trade I've made in a while," he said.

"Haven't seen you around," the soldier said. "What brings you to Fort Gibson?"

"Looking for the garrison commander," Slocum said. "I need to go through a stack of wanted posters."

The soldier blew a large smoke cloud and then spat. "Been a run on looking through the circulars. You're the second to look in the past week."

From the way the man spoke, Slocum knew the identity of the other. He said, "His name wouldn't happen to have been Pisser Wingate, would it?"

"Big son of a bitch. Bigger'n any man ought to be. Claimed to be an ex-lawman from up St. Louis way. No man in his right mind would dispute that."

"You don't happen to remember the wanted posters he looked at?" Slocum asked.

"I'm only a buck private. Can't say about such matters. You'd have to take that up with Captain Hawkins." The soldier blew a smoke ring that rose on the cool air, hung suspended for a moment, then tore apart when the wind caught it.

"Where do I find Hawkins?"

"He's always at the garrison. Never saw a man more devoted to serving his country." The hint of sarcasm along with a faint Southern accent alerted Slocum.

"You in the Army long?"

"Been up and down in rank a half-dozen times. Can't get nowhere on account of me being a former Reb. Wouldn't stay in, but what else do I know how to do?" He lifted one eyebrow and studied Slocum more carefully. "If memory serves, and it usually does, I seen you in these here parts before. Or maybe it was farther north, up in Kansas."

Slocum fell silent as he smoked. He had ridden with Quantrill's Raiders during the latter days of the war. It wasn't anything to be proud of, and he wasn't. They had gut-shot him and left him for dead when he protested their bloody-handed ways. That had been the way Quantrill and Bloody Bill Anderson and the others worked.

And John Slocum had held his own with them for more than a year until the Lawrenceville raid and his protests.

"Yep, reckon I have." The soldier hiked his feet to the railing and stared into space. "Don't have any love for Hawkins, and it's been too long since I went home to Pascagoula."

"Thought you were from the Deep South," said Slocum, still wondering if the soldier wanted to turn him in for some reward that might still be on his head.

"Too bad Quantrill got killed in '65. Could have used a man like him around here after the war."

Slocum didn't answer that. He had his own opinion of Quantrill and his vicious guerrilla band. When he said nothing, the soldier went on, as if he had spoken and agreed.

"Might have been him what pulled the bank robbery a few days back. Daring, quick, bloody. That's got Captain Hawkins in a real uproar, it has."

"Bank robbery?" Slocum tried not to sound too curious. "When was this?"

"A few days back, like I said. Must have been a Tuesday."

Slocum nodded and thought hard. He had joined Jethro August's wagon train on Wednesday—and the mysterious rider wearing the canvas duster might have been riding down from Fort Gibson and the bank robbery. He couldn't know for sure, but it explained why the man didn't want to take credit for saving the Throckmortons from the Choctaw braves. A bag filled with greenbacks might prove hard to explain, even to a pair of honest, relieved sodbusters.

Slocum smiled wryly. The rider might have thought he was the law. Who else would tangle with a band of Indian raiders to save a pair of greenhorns?

Before he could ask any questions of the trooper, the man shot to his feet and tossed his quirly into a watering trough. "Hot damn, here comes Captain Hawkins now." With that, the man disappeared into the general store. Slocum heard footsteps on the board flooring and then the slam of a back door.

The officer rode by, turned and saw Slocum, then reined about. "Have you seen a private loitering around here in the past few minutes?" he called out.

Slocum considered the question, puffed once, and said, "Can't say that I have, Captain."

The officer grunted and started on his way.

Slocum stopped him. "I need to go through your wanted posters. And if you've got a minute, I'd like to know what you've found out about the bank robbery last Tuesday."

"How is it you, a stranger, know about that?" Captain Hawkins asked suspiciously. He eyed Slocum as he tried to put a name to the face. "Who the hell are you?"

"Name's Slocum. I'm with Jethro August's wagon train heading up from the Illinois River area. We had a mite of trouble with robbers and thought we might get an idea who they were."

"Report your problems to my adjutant. I have to track down the bank robbers you asked after. We finally got a trail to follow. Good day, sir." Hawkins put his heels to his big black stallion's flanks and raced off.

"Thanks, mister," came the whisper from beside the

general store. Slocum turned to see the private. "He's un-
bearable as hell when he starts on one of his 'for God,
country, and President' talks."

"You supposed to be with him on this manhunt?" Slocum asked.

"Hell, I'm supposed to be in the galley fixing supper.
They busted me that far down." The soldier came out and
then blanched. "Shit, I gotta go. There. That's him again.
The one you was asking about. The bounty hunter asking
after the outstanding warrants." The private vanished once
more, heading back to the wood-walled stockade at the end
of the street.

Slocum turned and saw Pisser Wingate walking into
town, his saddle and gear slung over his shoulder. Of the
bounty hunter's horse he saw no trace. Deciding that he
had no reason to pick a fight with the mountain of a man,
Slocum sauntered into the general store and replenished the
foodstuffs he had used on the trail.

His canned goods slung in a burlap bag over his
shoulder, he went back out into the street and stashed his
purchases in his saddlebags. Of Wingate he saw nothing.
Not counting on luck, he slipped the leather thong off his
Colt Navy and followed the private's footsteps to the high
wooden walls of Fort Gibson.

From inside the stockade he heard Wingate roaring,
"Another goddamn robbery! The hell you say it was a gang
of three men. I *know* who done it. It was William Deutsch,
that's who done it. I'm gonna have that son of a bitch's
scalp or know the reason why."

Slocum turned left under the walkway and headed for
the adjutant's office. Pisser Wingate kept the soldiers busy
on the far side of the stockade near the lockup. He looked
over his shoulder several times to be sure the bounty hunter
didn't catch sight of him. After the way he'd left Wingate

dangling from the hickory tree, his name would be mud—
or worse.

The lieutenant sitting behind the adjutant's small drop-
leaf desk glanced up. "What can I do for you?" he asked.

"These look to be what I need," Slocum said, seeing the
pile of wanted posters held down with a large brass cartridge paperweight.

"That must be 'bout the most popular diversion in all
Fort Gibson these days," the adjutant said, leaning back in
his creaking chair. "We're getting a regular parade through
here looking at them."

"You might save me some time. Pisser Wingate—"

"That . . ." The adjutant bit back his curse. "I heard him
roaring and carrying on outside just now. I thought we'd
seen the last of him when he went off on his wild goose
chase a few weeks back."

"Looking for William Deutsch?"

"That's the name. Froze in my mind, it did," the lieutenant said. "Never saw a man carry on like Wingate did.
He had an old, battered wanted poster that's good for nothing, as far as I'm concerned. An old one, it was. I swear,
the poster went back to St. Louis well nigh ten years ago.
Deutsch is hardly a name on everyone's lips. Wingate tried
to convince me he had found a newer one in my stack, but
I ordered the sentry to toss him out. I had work to do, and
he was gettin' downright aggravating about it."

"Wingate thinks he pulled the bank robbery?"

"Might be; probably wasn't. Bank robbin's not unusual
in these parts, but it took a sight of daring to do it under
Captain Hawkins's nose. Pissed him off, it did."

The lieutenant turned back to his work while Slocum
thumbed through the posters. The torn, grease-stained one
fell out of the stack. Slocum didn't have to ask the lieutenant to know Pisser Wingate had studied this one real hard.

And he remembered now where he had seen Cole Mason before.

The bounty hunter had been right about the robber being on the wagon train. Mason and William Deutsch were one and the same man.

5

Slocum mounted his sorrel and started back for the wagon
train. He had gone only five miles when he heard the
thunder of hooves along the road ahead of him. He had
nothing to fear on a publicly traveled road, but the number
of horses approaching warned him that caution was prefer-
able to risk. Seeing a stand of elm and oak trees, he guided
his horse toward the sheltering darkness beneath them. The
sun was setting and cast long, dark shadows to shield him
from prying eyes.

He had less than five minutes to wait until the column of
cavalry passed by. The setting sun shone off their brass
uniform buttons and the bugle flopping up and down on the
leading rider's saddle. It took Slocum several seconds to
find the officer in charge. When he did, he recognized him
immediately.

"So Captain Hawkins caught his prey," Slocum said
aloud. He patted the sorrel's neck. The officer and six

horse soldiers rode in a ring around their prisoner. They passed by so quickly Slocum had no chance to see whom they had netted.

"Jethro's waiting for us back at the wagon train," he said to his horse. "We've got to tell him about the easy fords we found. He's going to be fit to be tied if we don't show up soon. And he *is* paying us well for scouting."

Slocum considered this, then urged his horse back along the road to Fort Gibson. He had to see if Captain Hawkins had Cole Mason as his prisoner. Slocum wasn't sure what he'd do if he had.

What did he owe the fake preacher? What did he owe Grace?

They had enjoyed each other's company from midnight till dawn, and he couldn't rightly remember a night more pleasurably spent with a woman. But should he try to rescue her father from the Fort Gibson lockup? Slocum decided he didn't owe her *that* much, but he wasn't about to let Cole Mason—or William Deutsch—end up in Pisser Wingate's custody. The bounty hunter would as soon return his prisoner dead as alive to St. Louis.

It wasn't so much for Grace or Cole Mason that he was returning but for the sake of keeping Wingate away from his prey. He had taken a powerful dislike to the bounty hunter.

Slocum arrived in Fort Gibson ten minutes after the hard-riding soldiers had entered the stockade. Many tended their horses, rubbing them down and getting rid of the lather flecking their sides. Captain Hawkins had ridden his troop hard.

Looking around and listening hard failed to reveal Pisser Wingate. Slocum dismounted and tethered his horse outside the fort's gate and walked inside. To his surprise,

Captain Hawkins's prisoner was not Cole Mason—or William Deutsch.

"This the owlhoot who robbed your bank?" Slocum asked a soldier standing guard beside the gate.

"Captain reckons he is. He surely does answer to the description of the leader. They lost the other two. They proved to be slipperier than greased pigs."

"Captain Hawkins isn't happy about that," Slocum said, more to himself than to the guard.

"He's madder'n a wet hen over it," the young guard agreed.

"Let's see what can be done." Slocum had no intention of getting tangled up in this. The officer had his bank robber, and it wasn't the preacher. Slocum knew he should get back on his horse and return to the wagon train, but too many unanswered questions piqued his curiosity. He decided a few more minutes spent feeding his interest in this wouldn't trouble him any.

"You," came the sharp word. "Stop. I know you. You were on the steps of Parson's store earlier this afternoon."

"I was, Captain," Slocum agreed. "I represent Jethro August's wagon train."

The prisoner jerked upright and stared straight at Slocum.

"What do you know of this man?" demanded Hawkins.

"I reckon he might have been with the train earlier on, but he was arrested for bank robbery back in Arkansas," Slocum said, taking a shot in the dark. From the prisoner's reaction when he mentioned Jethro's name, he had to be one of the three men hell-bent on making a name for themselves holding up banks.

"I don't remember you being with the train," the prisoner said.

Slocum tried to recollect the names of the three. He

couldn't. "I was hired to replace the three of you."

Captain Hawkins motioned for Slocum to join them in his small office. The officer pushed around and sat down in a chair the twin to the adjutant's. He adjusted his sword and finally took it from the leather hanger and laid it across his desk. "You don't deny robbing the Fort Gibson bank?" he asked of his prisoner.

"You know we did it, Captain. I don't see any reason to lie about it."

Hawkins looked from his prisoner to Slocum, who only shrugged. He hadn't thought the man would admit to guilt so easily.

"We'll get a judge in here within a week and send you to the Detroit Penitentiary, that I promise you."

"Got out of worse jails," the prisoner said sullenly.

"Captain, let me talk with him a few minutes. Mr. August would certainly appreciate it."

"There's nothing he can tell you," Hawkins said. To his prisoner he said, "Tell me where the other two are. We lost their trail ten miles to the south."

"They'll be damned hard to find," the man said. "I wish you luck."

"You'll be convicted for crimes they've committed," the officer said. "You'll be sent to jail while they're spending your money. Do you want it that way?"

"Better that two of us get to spend the money than none. They're my friends."

Slocum hardly believed this. There was no honor among thieves. Captain Hawkins simply hadn't tried the right tack in getting his prisoner to peach on the other two men.

"Stay with him a moment," Hawkins said, seeing that Slocum might get more information out of the man than he ever could. The captain gestured, and the soldier standing just inside the door moved away and trailed behind the officer.

Slocum closed the door and sat on the corner of the desk.

"You come to get me out. Brighton and Villalobos sent you, didn't they?" the man said hopefully.

Brighton. Villalobos. Slocum remembered the third man's name then: Dantley.

"No, Dantley," he said. "They didn't have the time. I *do* work for Jethro August. He's mighty sore at how you made him look bad pulling those robberies. He thought he left you behind. How did you ever get free of the law?"

"The boss fixed it for us. We escaped."

Slocum started to speak, then bit back the words. Dantley had added something he had only suspected. "The one in the canvas duster and the red bandanna is the leader?" he asked.

"You know a lot more'n you're letting on, mister. What do you want from me?"

"You pulled a passel of robberies," Slocum started.

"Seven," Dantley interrupted. "We done seven, and they all went smoother'n silk. Brighton talked me into doing this one without the boss. We done it just right, just as if . . ." He suddenly fell silent.

"Your leader didn't plan this one for you?"

"We got away from the law according to plan over in Arkansas, but we got separated. Brighton thought we could pull a robbery on our own."

"And not split it four ways?"

"Hell, the boss kept half. We divvied the rest among ourselves," Dantley said. "That's why we thought we could take a bank here and keep it all."

Slocum saw that planning wasn't Dantley's distinction.

He doubted the other two did much better. They had used an old plan laid out for them by the bandanna-wearing mastermind and it hadn't worked. Captain Hawkins had proven too diligent in his duty.

No one acted up in Fort Gibson without paying the price for it.

"Getting across the river to the south must have been hard, loaded down with so much money."

"We didn't have any problem," Dantley said. "We didn't get that much. The whole take fit into one damned small canvas bag. Brighton bitched about it, saying we'd got less than two hundred dollars. I thought it was more, but it's hard to say. We never had the chance to count it."

Slocum nodded. He had a good idea where Brighton and Villalobos had headed. Hawkins had given up his hunt for the others too soon. If he had kept after them, he'd have caught them before another day was out.

"William Deutsch," he said, studying Dantley's reaction. Only a moment of confusion showed. "You know him as Cole Mason. Tell me about him."

"What's to tell? He's a boring preacher man." Dantley got a sly expression on his face. Slocum wished he could play poker with this man. It would keep him in money for months. "What's the preacher got to do with this?"

"Nothing," Slocum said, sure now he knew who the mastermind behind the string of bank heists was. Reading Dantley's reaction was easier than reading a book.

He left Dantley and went to Captain Hawkins.

The Army officer stood impatiently waiting for Slocum's report. "Well?" he demanded. "What did you learn from him?"

"You gave up the hunt too soon. The other two were nearby."

"We lost their trail. We had no desire to hunt futilely forever. They're good trailsmen, all three of them."

"Probably so. He doesn't show any contrition. He just seems pissed that they didn't pull off the robbery any better than they did."

Slocum saw no reason to tell the officer about Cole Mason—or William Deutsch. He smiled wryly as he tipped his hat and left the angry officer. The reason he'd remembered Deutsch's face was the poster it had been nailed up next to: his. That had been a good twelve years back, when the hunt was still feverish for him on the judge-killing charges. That had died down, but enough others accumulated to make it dangerous for Slocum to stay here much longer.

The adjutant—or Captain Hawkins or even Pisser Wingate—might take it into their heads to go back through even older posters and find his smeary picture staring up at them.

"I'll check on your Mr. August's wagon train," Hawkins called out.

"We'll be much obliged, Captain. Those settlers need all the protection they can get, what with bank robbers and Choctaw raiding parties everywhere we turn."

The officer sputtered something Slocum didn't catch. His mind was already on Brighton and Villalobos. They might be good at concealing their trail; Hawkins and his men might be good at tracking. No matter what, John Slocum was better than both groups.

Where he expected to find the two men lay in the direction of the wagon train. The area around the river where the Throckmortons had been attacked couldn't be too far from the robbers' meeting spot. Slocum figured the newly escaped owlhoots might have had help from their boss—

and had double-crossed him with their Fort Gibson robbery. If so, they had met near where the sodbusters had
been attacked by the Indian raiding party.

He rode hard, not wanting to be gone from the wagon
train longer than he had to. After all, Jethro paid him to
scout, not do the cavalry's work for them. Still, curiosity
burned at him—and an anger at Pisser Wingate grew. The
man was too set on bringing in William Deutsch. Slocum
had seen bounty hunters like Wingate before and had hated
every one of them. They were cruel, vicious men who
thought nothing of snuffing out a life for a few dollars.
Slocum had lived like that when he rode with Quantrill,
hating every instant of it—and had had men of Wingate's
ilk on his trail.

That was a fate to be avoided. He knew he could simply
tell Cole Mason, but what would this do to Grace? She was
no shrinking violet, but finding that her father robbed
banks when he wasn't preaching wouldn't set well with
her. Slocum wanted to protect her from that knowledge if
he could.

All night he rode cross-country, and by dawn he came to
the area where he had rescued the Throckmortons. He ignored the spot where the sodbusters' wagon had been
mired. He concentrated on the patch of woods where he
had sighted the mysterious rider in the tan canvas duster.

The wind and a recent rain shower had obliterated any
clues he might have found. A small red thread still dangled
from a thorny bush where the rider had passed by and tangled the bandanna, but this didn't help him determine
where Cole Mason had come from before helping the
Throckmortons with his expert marksmanship.

Slocum determined the direction taken by the sodbusters, by the Indians where he had come upon them. What

remained had to be the direction from which Mason had ridden. He mounted and by searching ever-widening circles back and forth across the path likely taken by Mason finally found spoor.

Slocum began tracking in earnest, confident that he had hit on the right trail. He almost crowed in triumph when he came across a grassy area cut up by several horses' hooves. At least three riders had met here and discussed something for some time without dismounting. A bit more work on his part revealed the trail taken by at least two riders getting to the meeting point.

By noon he topped a rise and saw a thin column of wood smoke rising from a meadow.

He had no intention of boldly riding up to find out if the men cooking on this fire were Brighton and Villalobos. They might be spooked because of what had happened to Dantley.

Slocum frowned as the thought occurred to him that the two fugitives ought to be hightailing it for Mexico. Why stay behind when Dantley had been caught? Or did they even know? Slocum couldn't imagine robbers waiting for long to divvy up their take.

A new thought formed. They might be waiting for Cole Mason. He had met with them before. He might be ready to launch them at still another bank. Did Mason know his henchmen had been at work on their own in Fort Gibson?

Slocum shook his head. His curiosity had carried him this far, but there were too many facts to be learned. He ought to wheel about and return to the wagon train. This was none of his business.

Even as the notion of leaving Brighton and Villalobos occurred to him, he saw a rider in the distance. He sat motionless on his sorrel, watching the small brown dot grow larger. He wasn't unduly surprised when he saw the tips of a red bandanna fluttering in the wind and a canvas duster flapping around the smallish rider's body.

Slocum smiled as he followed the rider toward the distant meadow. His curiosity would soon be satisfied.

6

Slocum dismounted and tethered his horse to a blackberry bush a quarter mile away from his quarry and advanced on foot. He kept his Colt Navy in its holster. He wanted only to spy, not engage in a shoot-out. Captain Hawkins was the only lawman in these parts, and Slocum wasn't about to do his job for him. After he saw Cole Mason with Brighton and Villalobos, his curiosity would be satisfied. What preacher wanted it known that he also robbed banks?

Slocum wondered what he would tell Grace Mason about her father. She ought to know he was robbing banks, but Slocum wasn't sure it was his place to tell her. What did he owe her? They'd had a nice night together. She had surprised him with her sexual hunger. The fire had burned bright in both of them, and she had helped stoke it to a blaze in surprising ways that delighted him.

But did he owe her anything more? Should he even get

involved with the bogus preacher? Those were questions he didn't have easy answers for.

As he neared the meadow where Brighton and Villa-lobos had camped, he dropped into a crouch. The under-brush proved thicker than he'd thought from his cursory, distant observation. The going got harder—and thornier. Brambles caught at his shirt and denims. Slocum finally dropped to his belly and wiggled forward, beginning to wonder if this was necessary. His curiosity had gotten him into trouble before. Now he risked scratches and a possible bullet in the head if discovered—and for what?

Just as he was about to cash it in, he heard two voices drifting on the wind. One—it had to be Mason—was muffled and indistinct. Another man, this one speaking halting English, he reckoned to be Villalobos. The two robbers were arguing over something. Slocum worked closer to find out what.

". . . should have helped us out of the prison instead of letting us rot," said Villalobos angrily. The man stood with his hands on his hips, his fingers drumming constantly on an intricate silver conch belt that reminded Slocum of Jethro August's hatband. They might have been hammered out by the same Taxco silversmith. Partially hidden by the Mexican was Cole Mason. The man stood with his ban-danna pulled up under his chin, his lower face mostly hid-den. The way he had his hat brim pulled down and veiled in shadow made positive identification impossible. He wore the same tan canvas duster Slocum had seen him wearing when he had aided the mired-down sodbusters.

To one side stood a third man. Slocum guessed this si-lent, stolid man was Brighton.

Slocum wiggled to his right to get a better view of Mason. Something about the short preacher worried Slo-cum. The way he stood struck him as wrong. The harder

Slocum tried to figure what struck him as wrong, the less sure he was.

His chambray shirt caught on a bramble and rattled still-dry leaves. Slocum froze as the men turned, quick hands flashing to their holstered guns.

"What was that?" demanded Brighton.

"Quièn está? Who is it?" called Villalobos.

Slocum cursed under his breath as he tried to get free of the thorny shrub. Part of his shirt tore away. The ripping sound carried in the Oklahoma stillness. Villalobos and Brighton both drew their six-shooters. Mason reached under the duster and dragged out a sawed-off shotgun.

The pistols Slocum faced with little fear. More men carried them than could use them well. Too few properly oiled and loaded their side arms as he did. The Colt Navy still in his holster was a precision tool and more accurate than either of these bank robbers' pistols. The scattergun worried the hell out of him, though. A wild shot might cut off his legs. A well-placed one could cut him in half.

It was damned near impossible to miss with such a vicious weapon. His only hope lay in putting enough distance between himself and the muzzle. Although the shotgun was deadly, it had no range.

"To hell with it," Slocum said, trying to keep his voice down. He grunted and ripped both shirt and flesh. Brighton opened fire at the sound, a heavy slug sinking into the soft dirt two feet from Slocum's head. He jerked away from the point of impact and scuttled into the thicket.

He made too much noise. Villalobos opened up with his pistol, and then Slocum's worst fears were realized. The sawed-off shotgun roared. Heavy buckshot tore through the brush. He felt a hot pain lance across his cheek. Reaching up, he touched his cheek and his fingers came away bloody.

"Damn!" Slocum began crawling faster. The outlaws' six-shooters barked repeatedly, but they had no clear target. The slugs passed by harmlessly and whined into the woods.

By the time he got to his feet, Slocum thought he was safe. A twig cracking made him freeze. He looked over his left shoulder and saw Mason standing, the red bandanna pulled up over his nose and the battered brown hat brought down so that it hid even his eyes. He had fastened the duster, but the scattergun was out and leveled at Slocum's belly.

Slocum waited to die. He watched as the finger tightened on the double triggers. Then the bank robber spun and vanished like smoke into the forest.

"Wait!" Slocum called out. He didn't understand why he was still alive. Mason had had a clear shot. At this range the buckshot from the shotgun would have blown him into bloody shreds.

Why hadn't the robber fired when he had a chance? To that Slocum had no answer, but he was thankful. He had been careless, and Mason had let him live. Slocum wasn't going to look a gift horse in the mouth, but he wondered at the man's reasoning. If he had discovered anyone spying on him like he had been, Slocum knew he would have fired without hesitation.

Common sense dictated that he hightail it for his horse and let the bank robbers finish their business. Curiosity burned inside him, though. Why hadn't Mason cut him down when he had the chance?

Slocum circled and came back to the meadow from a different direction. The brambles still tore at his clothing, but this time he ignored them. His shirt hung in tatters, and his torso was crisscrossed with shallow cuts. The worst wound, though, was the superficial crease on his right cheek. The channel left by the buckshot burned like hell-fire. Slocum knew he'd have to get it tended to soon or it would become infected. Mason's buckshot had probably been lubricated with rancid lard.

As this thought crossed his mind, Slocum stopped and sniffed at the spring Oklahoma air. A familiar stench filled his nostrils. He hadn't pulled his Colt before. He did so now.

Dropping onto his belly, he inched forward to see what was happening in the clearing. Before he could yell out a warning to Villalobos, the Mexican died. Pisser Wingate had crept up behind the robber on cat's feet. A thick-bladed knife flashed in the syrupy warm sunlight and drove hard and deep into the man's back until the bloody steel tip came out his chest.

Slocum fired at the bounty hunter, but the mountain of a man moved faster than any human he'd ever seen. Wingate rolled to his left and came to his feet, knife still in his left hand. With his meaty right, he reached out and caught Brighton's gun hand. Fingers crushing the robber's wrist, Wingate lifted.

Brighton screamed. Wingate's bowie knife came up and stopped just under the man's uplifted, stubbled chin. Slocum saw a thin line of red appear as the bounty hunter pressed the razor-sharp edge into taut, exposed flesh.

Slocum sighted carefully and squeezed the trigger. He stopped when Wingate swung about, putting Brighton between them. Slocum had no compunction about killing Brighton, too. The man was a bank robber and had probably killed in cold blood. But Slocum couldn't get Mason's strange charity out of his head. The robbers' leader had had the chance to kill him and hadn't.

He looked for Mason, thinking the masked preacher might come to Brighton's rescue. No trace of the man remained. When he had vanished into the dense forest, he must have gone directly to his horse, mounted, and ridden away like the wind. By the time Wingate appeared, Mason was long gone.

Brighton screamed again. Slocum's attention fixed once more on the bounty hunter and his captive. He shuddered when he saw what Wingate was doing. Slocum had seen Plains Indians use the same technique on captured cavalry troopers. The tip of the bowie knife cut open the skin; the blade peeled it back with a single slow movement. Wingate was skinning the man alive.

"Tell me, damn your eyes. Tell me where he is! I want William Deutsch!"

Brighton moaned something incoherent. Wingate continued using the knife to peel back skin while he held the man's wrists together in a single huge right hand.

Slocum wasn't going to stand about and watch even an escaped robber be tortured to death. He didn't know Brighton or owe him anything, but he had nothing against bank robbery. He had done a mite of it in his time. No robber deserved this kind of slow and agonizing death.

"Stop it, Wingate!" he bellowed. A shot from his six-shooter passed a few inches above the bounty hunter's head.

Wingate swung around, bloody knife in his hand. He roared like a wounded grizzly and stood. "Who is it? That you, boy? The one what gave me so much trouble back at the wagon train? What's your interest in this piece of trash? He was fixin' to tell me where Deutsch is."

"Turn him over to Captain Hawkins." Slocum had no fondness for bounty hunters. Pisser Wingate's behavior made him sick to his stomach. Putting a bullet in the man's thick head would be a service.

"I ain't got the time. I want William Deutsch." Wingate

cocked his head to one side. "You tied in with these vermin? Is that what's got your tail all tied up in a knot?"

Wingate stepped away from Brighton. "Yeah, I'm beginning to think you're in this up to your ears. I don't rightly remember seein' your picture on a wanted poster, but I reckon there must be a price on you from somewhere."

Slocum knew then that he'd have to kill Wingate. He couldn't allow the man to find out about the dead carpetbagger judge back in Georgia. The reward wasn't much, but it didn't take much to tempt a bounty hunter like Wingate. He was a cruel, murderous son of a bitch that needed stopping.

Slocum lifted his Colt and fired. Wingate roared in pain as the bullet struck him squarely in the middle of the chest. He staggered, but it would take more than a single .38 slug to slow him. Slocum fired again. This time he missed.

Wingate's incredible speed allowed him to dodge to one side, throwing off Slocum's aim. In the same sideways move, Wingate tossed his knife. Slocum saw a silver cartwheel coming at him. He moved in time to keep the blade from sinking hilt-deep in his belly. He held down the red-hot wave of pain from the slash it left in his side as it passed.

"You move good for a little fella," Wingate complimented. From somewhere in the depths of his dirty buckskins he pulled out a knife that was a twin to the one that had almost gutted Slocum.

Slocum fired again. Wingate took a second slug. The impact rocked the bounty hunter back on his heels but didn't stop him. Slocum lifted his aim, thinking to put a bullet into the man's head. He hesitated. He had fired point-blank at a grizzly once. The bullet had struck squarely between the hulking black beast's eyes—and ricocheted. The bear's skull had been so thick it took the full force of a bullet, even at close range.

The instant's hesitation allowed Wingate to close the distance between them. Slocum's head filled with flashing impressions. He heard Brighton moaning in pain a dozen paces away. He heard the crashing of Wingate's feet pounding on the ground. His body burned from buckshot and knife wounds. Then the reeking bounty hunter's odor blotted out everything else.

Slocum and Pisser Wingate locked together and fell to the ground. The impact knocked the breath from Slocum's lungs. Gasping, he tried to get free. The bounty hunter pinned him securely to the ground. Wingate towered above him, a hulk of gristle and meanness. The thick-bladed bowie knife gleamed wickedly in the sunlight as he lifted it for the killing stroke.

Slocum's numb fingers tightened on the trigger of his the six-shooter, and he felt it buck. Wingate winced but showed no sign of being seriously injured by the shot.

"This'll learn you not to meddle where you don't belong, boy." The knife came rushing down. Slocum grunted and shoved to one side. The steel blade plunged into the soft dirt where his throat had been a fraction of a second earlier.

Struggle as he might, though, he couldn't move Wingate off him. The man's leg pinned his gun hand to the ground, and firing a second time had no effect. Even worse than the crushing weight was the odor. Wingate let off a stench worse than any skunk.

"You're feisty for one so tiny. Ain't gonna do you no good. You're dead meat, boy."

Slocum tried to lift Wingate straight up and turn him over. He failed. Then came the roar of a shotgun.

Wingate's weight vanished.

For several seconds Slocum lay flat on his back, stunned. The wind slowly filtered back into his heaving lungs, and the air revived him painfully.

He sat up, Colt held in a trembling hand. Across the clearing he saw Wingate charging into the forest. A bull's roar followed another shotgun blast.

Slocum tried to get off a shot at the man's receding back and failed. He sank to the ground for a few more seconds, then heaved himself erect. Every bone in his body ached. The gash on his side oozed blood, and his legs wobbled as he walked.

He went to Brighton's side. The man stared up at him, his eyes glazing over with death.

Slocum looked up from the partially skinned man to the forest where Wingate had rushed off after Cole Mason. He steadied, and he knew what had to be done. No matter what the preacher man had done, either as William Deutsch or Cole Mason, he didn't deserve the same fate as Villalobos and Brighton.

Slocum vowed to end Pisser Wingate's life, for his own satisfaction more than anything else.

7

John Slocum shook himself like a wet hound dog and tried to clear his vision. The brief, deadly fight with Pisser Wingate had taken too much out of him. He had to go to earth and recover his senses. Just sucking in a deep breath sent pain racing through his body.

Clutching his side, he turned from the partially skinned Brighton and went into the dense copse, intending to find his horse and get the hell away from the bounty hunter. Cole Mason might not have taken his life when he had the chance, but Slocum wasn't going to return the favor by tracking down Wingate and back-shooting the man. Let the bounty hunter and the bank-robbing preacher shoot it out. The way Slocum felt, they deserved each other.

He heard his sorrel whinnying in the distance. His already long stride lengthened when he heard the distress in the horse's cries, then shortened until he came to a complete stop. The horse wasn't skittish usually. Why was it

raising such a ruckus? He dropped to one knee and took the
time to reload his six-shooter. Although Wingate had taken
off in the opposite direction after Mason, he moved faster
than any man Slocum had ever seen.

Colt Navy in his right hand and his left holding the
wound in his side together, Slocum advanced cautiously. It
saved his life. At first he saw nothing. Then the wind
changed and blew into his face. The stench spooking his
horse now caused his nostrils to widen. Pisser Wingate was
somewhere close by.

Green eyes panning slowly across the brambles and
trees around the area where his horse reared and pawed,
Slocum finally spotted a dark lump at the base of a large
oak. At first he thought it was only a trick of shadow. Then
it moved and he saw the glint of sunlight off the thick-
bladed bowie knife Wingate used.

Slocum cursed softly. Had the bounty hunter already
killed Mason? It looked that way. Otherwise, why bother to
come after him? There didn't seem to be anything in the
entire world Wingate wanted more than Mason's—or William Deutsch's—scalp.

Slocum considered his chances of making a clean shot
into the shifting shadows by the tree bole. He decided he'd
prefer using a rifle. He looked at his horse and the Winchester carbine shoved into a saddle sheath. If he walked
over to the horse, pretending not to hurry or notice the
smell on the wind, he might be able to get the rifle free,
cocked, and ready for use on Wingate.

And then again, in his condition, he might not. Slocum
didn't dare forget how blindingly fast Pisser Wingate was.
One mistake and he would end up as dead as Villalobos
and Brighton.

Slocum decided against retrieving the rifle, even though
he needed its stopping power. He had hit Wingate at least

twice in the chest, and the bounty hunter hadn't noticed. A
third slug might have ripped into the man's leg. When he
went tearing off after Mason, there hadn't been any sign of
a limp. The man was more than human. He was a natural
force, like a tornado.

Deciding on the best tactic to use cost Slocum the element of surprise. Wingate sighted him. There was no sub-
tlety in the bounty hunter's attack. He lowered his head,
roared deep in his throat, and charged like a bull.

He erupted from the shadows and raced directly across
the open ground toward Slocum. The wounded man lifted
his Colt and sighted. One shot. He hit the running man.
Two shots. One missed, the other ripped off a bit of fringe
on Wingate's left arm. Two more shots. One hit a hard-
pumping leg and brought the bounty hunter to the ground.
The other was a clean miss.

Slocum had one shot left, and he intended to use it well.
He advanced and aimed directly at Wingate's head. Even
though he remembered what had happened when he'd fired
at the grizzly bear, he was willing to see if it didn't at least
stun Wingate. Just as his finger came back, Wingate
lurched and drove his knife at Slocum's leg.

His reaction was involuntary. Slocum jerked away—
and his shot missed Wingate's head by more than a foot.
He yelled in rage and pain when the sharp edge cut through
his denims and across his upper thigh. A new river of
blood stained his clothing. Worse than the wound was the
knowledge that he had emptied the last cylinder of his six-
shooter.

All he had to use against the man-mountain was the
knife he kept sheathed at the small of his back. Slocum
danced away the best he could and let Wingate fall flat on
his face. He holstered his Colt Navy and whipped out his
own knife.

Pisser Wingate smiled crookedly. "You got guts, boy. And I'm gonna spread 'em all over the forest. You're gonna be the most fun I've had in months."

Slocum didn't let Wingate get the upper hand. He attacked without returning the taunt. He had nothing to say; all he wanted to do was keep on living. Blade low and moving up in a deadly arc, Slocum cut at Wingate's arm. He had the range. Something went wrong with the delivery. He thought the tip of the knife turned off something hard under the bounty hunter's fringed buckskin sleeve.

Then he was too busy staying alive to worry about it. Wingate got his balance back. The shot to the leg hadn't slowed his incredible speed. He lunged, the tip of his bowie knife almost opening Slocum's belly, then followed with a rush, trying to get his arms around Slocum. This time Slocum sidestepped and let the bull of a man rush past.

Using his knife, Slocum raked Wingate's side. The bounty hunter yelled in rage. A thin trickle of blood sprang out to stain the battered buckskins.

"You're not gettin' away with this, boy. I'm gonna hurt you bad 'fore I kill you."

Slocum knew he couldn't match Wingate's strength in a protracted battle. He had shot all six rounds from his Colt, and reaching his Winchester was out of the question. But as he thought of the carbine, a smile crossed his lips. He swung his knife wildly, keeping Wingate at bay and making the man think he had panicked.

"I got you now, boy. You're dead."

Pisser Wingate rushed. Slocum sliced the sorrel's reins and sidestepped once more. The frightened horse reared and kicked out. The bounty hunter tried to avoid the hooves and failed. A sick crunch sounded as a front hoof struck his head.

Slocum watched the bounty hunter crumple to the ground. He felt no sense of triumph. He was alive, and that was all that mattered. Holding his side, he turned and went after his horse. It took several minutes to run the horse down. Five more minutes passed before the sorrel quieted enough for Slocum to mount and ride.

He turned back toward the wagon train. He had quite a report to give Jethro.

By the time he reached the wagons, he was on the verge of passing out.

"John!"

He almost kept riding, too far gone to respond to his name. Someone rode up and reached over, taking the reins from his fatigued hands. He turned to see who it was and almost fell out of the saddle. Strong hands held him upright.

"John, get down. I'm not strong enough to do it without dropping you."

"You're doing a right fine job," he said, still not focusing too well. "I'm burning up. Fever. Got an infected wound." He tried to touch his cheek to indicate where the preacher's buckshot had left a groove, but he knew it was his injured side that was causing him the most trouble.

"I can see that. You've been in one righteous fight, John. What happened?"

He fought to focus his eyes. He saw Grace Mason. In spite of her belief that she couldn't hold him, she was doing a good job. She was much stronger than she looked, her hands gripping the front of his shredded shirt as she held him against his horse.

"Ran afoul of a tornado."

"Bloodied you up, too. Come along. Let me tend those knife wounds. They don't look as bad as you make them out to be. You just want a bit of sympathy."

"No . . ." His denial fell on deaf ears.

"Over here. Papa's out preaching. He'll be gone for some time."

"Why isn't the wagon train moving along?"

"There's been some problem in Broken Arrow. The land recorder cannot give us the deeds to our land for another few days. Or that's what Mr. August told us. I think he's lying. There is something else holding us up."

Slocum said nothing. He had to report to the wagon-master before he found out firsthand what the problem was. He had expected the wagon train to be knocking on the door at Fort Gibson in a day or two. If Jethro kept the wagons here for three days, it meant more than not finding suitable fords across the river.

"I've got to see Jethro. He might be holding up the wagon train because of me." Slocum didn't think so, but Jethro was a cautious man—when he wasn't drunk.

"No, John," Grace Mason said softly. The strength in her hands pressing against his shoulders belied the tone she used. Velvet and steel, he thought suddenly. How little he knew of her. In that moment he knew she could take the bad news about her father. He might have told her he was out preaching up a storm of hellfire and threats of eternal damnation, but Slocum knew different. Cole Mason— William Deutsch—hadn't got back yet from the deadly encounter with Pisser Wingate.

He looked into her cornflower blue eyes and sagged. He didn't have the strength to argue. Or was it more?

She bent over and lightly kissed him. The weakness that had assailed him on his ride back vanished. He reached out and laced his fingers through her raven's-wing black hair and pulled her lips down to his. They kissed deeply, but she broke off.

"What's wrong?" he asked.

"I don't want you passing out on me," she said, almost primly. She reached around him and unerringly found the knife sheathed at the small of his back. She pulled it out with a practiced movement and began cutting off his shirt. He started to protest, then stopped. The chambray shirt had cost him four dollars, but it was ruined. What the thorns hadn't ripped, Wingate had slashed and bloodied with his vicious knife.

She got him naked to the waist and went to boil water. Slocum leaned back against the high wheel of the preacher's wagon and closed his eyes. He still hadn't decided what to tell Grace about her father.

He winced when she returned and gently soaked off the dirt and dried blood.

"That's a nasty wound. You should see a doctor about getting it stitched up. I could do it, but I've never been too good with a needle and thread."

"Try," Slocum said, staring at the knife wound. He saw she was right. The laceration was worse than he'd first thought.

"It'll hurt like hell," she said, smiling wickedly. "Hell is something I know all about." Grace ran her fingers over the other scars on Slocum's broad chest. "You must know about that too."

He nodded. He had seen his share of pain and injury and bloody death, both during the war and after.

"Let me work on this." Grace got needle and thread and ran the needle tip through the small fire she had used to boil water for cleaning the wound. Slocum closed his eyes and tried to think of more pleasant things when she began stitching up the gash. He found it easier to do than he'd thought possible. Grace kept running her free hand between his legs, squeezing gently, massaging, teasing.

"There," she said at last. "All done."

He reached out and caught her wrist. She pulled away easily, startling him. He hadn't realized he was so weak.

Slocum stood and found that he was steadier now than he had been before. Grace always managed to surprise him by being something more than he thought.

"You've still got a few wounds to tend," she said. "Let's go into the wagon where I can get at them better." She looked around to see if any of the others in the wagon train had overheard. None even took notice of them as they climbed in.

"Here," she said, patting the soft mattress spread in the center of the wagon. Her and her father's possessions rose up on either side. Slocum felt as if he had sneaked into a gopher hole. Then he forgot all about such notions.

Grace slid full-length next to him on the feather mattress, her mouth seeking his. She kissed and licked and nibbled at his face and ears and throat.

"Is this better than pouring hot water on your wounds?" she asked. Her eager fingers traced along the shallow crease in his cheek. He winced.

"Sorry," she said. "I didn't mean to hurt you. Is that from a piece of buckshot?"

"Reckon it is."

"Damnation, you surely do end up with a passel of injuries for a man going scouting in civilized territory." She slid away and came back with more of the hot water. She dabbed at his cheek. "This will fester if it's not properly tended. There'd have been pig fat on the buckshot for greasing, you know."

He looked at her strangely, then forgot all about anything but the warm, willing woman's body pressed so fervently against his. The aches and pains faded, and he forgot about the injuries he had accumulated.

Their mouths met and their hands explored. He found

the ties to Grace's dress and fumbled them open. Her bod-
ice parted and revealed twin mounds of creamy flesh. He
cupped her breasts, squeezing down slightly. She sighed
and leaned back on the feather mattress, looking for all the
world like a contented feline.

"Don't stop now, John. Keep going. I want so much
more." She grinned her wicked grin and reached out to
unbuckle his gunbelt and denims. "I want *this!*" She thrust
her hand down the front of his trousers and found the
straining pillar of manhood struggling to get free.

Her fingers stroked up and down until Slocum was
about ready to call out in frustration. She kissed him full
on the lips again and then rolled to one side. Somehow
Grace managed to come out of her blouse as she turned,
showing herself naked to the waist.

"More," she said in a husky whisper. "Take *everything* off
me." She wiggled her hips seductively. Slocum reached out
and helped her get free of her skirt. His hands lingered on the
twin peaks of her breasts, taking the coppery-colored nipples
between his fingers and rolling them around. He felt her heart
pounding. The nipples hardened as he tweaked them. Only
then did he rub gently down over the slightly curved dome of
her belly—and move even lower.

His fingers tangled in the damp fleece between her legs.
He found a moist slit and stroked over it. The preacher's
daughter gasped and thrust her hips downward until he
cupped her most intimate flesh.

"I want more, John, I want you, I want you now!"
Grace's voice took on a desperate note. He couldn't deny
her need. They both wanted the same thing.

Slocum shifted on the mattress and let the woman strad-
dle his waist. Her fingers caught at his erection and pulled
it in. They both gasped when she sank down, taking his
full length inside her. For a moment, Slocum was content

to simply lie back and let the sensations wash through his body like a fine warm spring rain.

Then the woman's hips began bucking and it was no longer enough for him to lie passively. He sat up, his arms circling her body. He pulled her close until her luscious breasts crushed flat against his chest. They kissed, their tongues dueling and dancing. All the while, Grace bounced up and down. Their crotches ground together, but it wasn't enough for John Slocum.

He bent forward, forcing Grace onto her back. She got her legs free and lifted them on either side of his body. In this position he was able to work out the rampaging desire burning in his loins.

"Fast, John, do it fast. I need you burning me up inside. Fast!" Grace locked her heels behind his back. Every forward thrust he made was doubled in power by the action of her legs. Slocum slid forward easily, then pulled back slowly.

Her body trembled in response to this teasing motion. She looked up at him, her eyes bright and bold. Arching her back, she kissed him. As she sagged back to the mattress, Slocum's hips thrust, driving her down even harder.

Grace gasped. Slocum thought he was going to explode when he felt her innards clamping down all around his hidden length. Her body trembled like a leaf in a high wind, and a bright flush crept up past her breast to her shoulders and neck. She tensed and relaxed, then urged him to keep moving.

"That's good, John. But I want more!"

"Greedy bitch!" he accused, forgetting she was a preacher's daughter. To his surprise, this made Grace even hotter. She clawed at him. Her body strained to melt into his, and her kisses turned even more fervent.

Locked together, they strove until Slocum no longer had

the control to hold back. The hot rush of his seed filled her and gave her another bout of trembling ecstasy.

Sweaty, they collapsed together onto the feather mattress. For several minutes neither said anything. They were content to lie with their arms around each other.

Slocum propped himself upon one elbow and looked down at her beautiful face. He stroked her cheeks and throat, then turned a bit more on the mattress.

"What's wrong, John?" she asked when he tensed.

Slocum saw a familiar red bandanna poking out from under the edge of the mattress on which they'd just made love. It was the same bandanna worn by her father just hours earlier.

8

"What is it?" Grace Mason asked.

"Just looking at this." Slocum pulled the dusty, sweat-stained red bandanna from under the mattress. It was identical to the one worn by Cole Mason.

"That's Papa's," she said, frowning. "Why are you looking at it as if you'd never seen one before? Everyone wears one to keep out the awful dust. Why, I've got one just like it I wear when the wagon train starts rolling. We crossed Arkansas, and the dust liked to have choked me it was so thick."

"How long has your father been out preaching?"

She shrugged, her lovely, bare shoulders shining white in the thin rays of sun poking past the wagon's canvas covering. Slocum found it hard to concentrate on anything but Grace. Her breasts bobbed slightly as she moved.

"He left an hour before you got here."

"An hour?"

"Maybe less. He . . . he came riding up hard and was all out of breath. He dismounted and didn't even give me a 'by-your-leave' he was in such a hurry."

"What was he wearing?"

"John, I don't think I like this. You're acting like a lawman." She tipped her head to one side, as if studying him critically. "You're not a law officer, are you?"

He laughed harshly at this notion. "Never even wanted to be," he admitted.

"Then why all the questions about Papa?"

For the hundredth time he wondered if he should tell her about the preacher's sideline business of robbing banks. He decided not to. He had upset her enough with questions about the bandanna. Slocum wasn't sure what he had been getting at, but the sight of the red neck scarf had caused him to speak without thinking.

"I've got to got talk with Jethro," he said, wiggling around to find his denims.

"Wait, John, don't go. You'll need a new shirt. I'll find one of Papa's for you to borrow."

He knew he couldn't go shirtless around the wagon train without causing a stir. Right now all he wanted to do was keep out of the sodbusters' rumor mill.

"Here's an old one he hardly ever wears. I hope it fits."

Slocum tried it on and found it too tight. Cole Mason was much smaller than he looked.

"Don't button it. The shoulders are too tight, but no one will notice until you get another shirt." Grace sat and shook her head. "You're so big and strong, John," she said. "Why, I can wear Papa's shirt and it fits me fine. But on you, it's far too tight for comfort."

He started to get into his denims, but Grace stopped him. "You're no lawman. You said so."

He stared into her bright blue eyes. They had a feverish

look to them, just as they did when she was making love.

"I'm not the law," he said. "I'm not much more than a scout helping out a friend."

"You know what happened to the other three men who rode scout for the wagon train?"

He nodded. He remembered the talk with Dantley—and the sight of Villalobos being cut down and Brighton skinned alive wouldn't fade soon from his memory.

"Well, they escaped," she said, almost breathlessly. "One of them is in the Fort Gibson jail."

"I heard," he said cautiously, not sure where she was leading. He wasn't sure he liked the flush coming to her cheeks. Something was exciting her as much as he had.

"The bank robber," Grace said in a rush. "Dantley. He's in the lockup. I . . . I'd like to see him. If I can't, would you talk to him for me?"

"What's this Dantley to you?" Slocum had an uneasy suspicion about Grace and the robber.

"I don't know how to tell you this, John. I mean, you'll get the wrong idea."

"You and he were lovers," Slocum said flatly.

"Gracious, no!" she exclaimed. "Nothing like that!"

The indignation in her voice erased the mistrust from his mind like morning sun causing the dew to disappear. No matter how good an actress, no woman could sound so aggrieved.

"This is truly embarrassing, though. Almost as much as if he and I had been . . ."

"What is it?" Slocum asked.

"Dantley is Papa's cousin. A black sheep in the family, to be sure. We were so disappointed in him when he and his two awful friends were arrested for robbing those banks."

"You want to talk with Dantley?"

"Or let you carry him a message letting him know that Papa forgives him. Sometimes I think Papa is too easygoing and forgiving with lawbreakers like Arlo Dantley, but then that's one reason I love him so much."

"That's all? Just tell Dantley that the preacher forgives him?"

"Tell him Papa forgives him for *all* his transgressions," she said, putting special emphasis on the word "all."

"Reckon I'll be going into town pretty soon for Jethro. I could drop by the Fort Gibson stockade and talk with him a few minutes." Something struck Slocum as wrong, and he couldn't tell what it was. He found himself looking constantly from her naked loveliness to the dirty bandanna lying on the wagon bed a yard away.

He didn't know why he didn't want to tell her he had already seen Dantley.

"Be sure to tell him that Papa will pray for *all* his sins on Sunday."

"All right," said Slocum, puzzled over her expression. She looked as if she was ready for another bout of lovemaking. Grace's face was flushed and her cheeks had turned rosy. Even her nipples had hardened again in excitement.

"You cotton to the notion of bank robbing?" Slocum asked.

"It's so . . . illegal," she said. "But there is something about it that I find romantic. I just wish Papa's cousin hadn't been caught at it. This shames him something fierce."

"I can understand that, him being a preacher and all," Slocum replied.

"After you talk with Arlo, let me know. I want to know how he's doing."

"Did Jethro know Dantley was a relation when he hired

the man? Or did your pa speak up for him out of the good-
ness of his heart?"

"Papa didn't know anything about Cousin Arlo applying
for the position with Mr. August," she said. "He said nothing, however, when he learned of it. As I said, Papa is a
forgiving man. He might have thought Cousin Arlo had
learned his lesson." Grace's voice dropped to a conspira-
torial whisper. "He served time up in the Detroit Penitentiary. It is truly the disgrace of the family."

Slocum almost laughed. If he hadn't finished off Pisser
Wingate, Cole Mason might have been doing time—or
been lucky even to get sentenced. The bounty hunter
wasn't the kind to arrive in court with many live prisoners.

"I'll see that Dantley gets the message."

"Thank you, John. You're such a good man." Grace
moved closer and kissed him.

For several seconds he thought about spending another
hour with her, but duty called louder than ever. He had to
find Jethro August and report. He also wanted to find out
why the wagon train hadn't budged in three days. As anxious as Jethro had been to deliver the sodbusters, it struck
Slocum as odd that they hadn't moved on sooner.

"I've got to go," he said, disengaging from the woman's
arms.

She smiled at him, a dreamy expression on her face.
"Don't be a stranger, John."

"Grace, your father's a preacher."

"And I'm a woman," she said, taking his hand and
placing it on one of her perfectly formed breasts. "What he
preaches has no bearing on what I feel—and need."

Slocum kissed her again, got his trousers fastened, and
slid from the wagon bed, his gunbelt slung over his
shoulder. Movement was restricted owing to the tight-
fitting shirt. He marveled at Grace's claim she could wear

her pa's clothing. He had to be damned careful not to lift his arm and tear out the seams in the armpits.

Slocum went directly to where he had left his small stash of clothing. He had only one spare shirt. If it hadn't been for his winning streak on the Mississippi riverboat, he wouldn't even have had a spare. He stripped off Mason's too-small shirt and donned his own. He'd have to return it later. First he had to find Jethro.

He made sure the soft leather cross-draw holster rode easy on his hip, then checked the load. He knew he ought to take the time to clean the cylinders and barrel but wanted to report to Jethro and find what was happening in the wagon train.

Slocum started off but hadn't gone a hundred yards through the camp when he heard Cole Mason's booming voice.

"We are all sinners!" he cried. "But there is salvation, if we will only wash ourselves in the blood of the Lamb!"

Slocum's steps turned in the direction of the small knot of sodbusters gathered around to listen. Mason heated up and finished with a flourish.

"Thank you, sinners and would-be saints. I will be happy to aid you in your search for eternal salvation. Please let me be of service to you." Most of the settlers drifted off. One or two lingered, then left when they saw that Slocum wanted to talk with the preacher.

"Mr. Slocum, you've returned from your sojourn," Mason said. "Does this mean the wagon train will finally move on into Broken Arrow? I am anxious to find a spot for a church. Nothing improves a congregation's lot more than knowing they have a permanent spot for Sunday services."

"I'm sure that's right," Slocum allowed. He looked around, not wanting to have this discussion if Grace was nearby, but the lovely darkhaired woman was nowhere to be seen.

"You know what you're doing, preacher?" asked Slocum.

"I hope so, sir," Mason said, startled. "I don't believe anyone has ever asked that of me before. I have studied for many years and preached diligently for the past ten. Although salvation is sometimes approached and often denied, I still seek it for my flock."

"That's not what I meant. You know Pisser Wingate, don't you?"

"The bounty hunter," Mason said, his voice suddenly neutral. Slocum wondered what playing poker with this man would be like.

"He was after a bank robber named William Deutsch."

"Mr. August told me this," Mason said. "What concern is it of mine?"

"Nothing," Slocum said. "Wingate is dead."

"A pity," Mason said, but his voice carried a lilt of joy. "A life wasted is a sorry thing."

"Do you think the same way about your cousin?"

"I'm sorry, sir. You talk in riddles. I don't have a cousin. My family is small and—"

"I meant Arlo Dantley."

"Dantley? Are you referring to the man arrested for bank robbery back in Arkansas?"

"He's your cousin, isn't he?"

"No." Mason's expression carried a mixture of confusion and irritation. "I just told you, I come from a small family. Dantley is no relation."

"Got confused. Thought I heard someone say you and he were related. I apologize for any distress my mistake caused you."

"Really, Mr. Slocum, you shouldn't listen to idle

rumors. There are pawns of Satan among the people of this wagon train. They might say and do outrageous things to keep me from spreading the word of God to those who need it most."

"I'll think twice before swallowing such a yarn again, preacher. Good day." Slocum touched his hat brim and started off, wondering about Mason. The man had shown definite signs of relief when he heard Wingate had died. On the other hand, he hadn't reacted as Slocum would have thought when Arlo Dantley's name was mentioned.

He shrugged it off. It must be as Grace had said: Cole Mason was embarrassed by a black sheep in the family— and one who had gotten caught so easily.

Slocum sauntered off, aware of Mason's eyes boring holes in his back. He ignored the preacher and kept walking, stopping only when he came to the Throckmorton wagon. The sodbuster and his domineering wife were working quietly, greasing the rear wheel of their wagon.

"Howdy, Mr. Slocum," the man greeted. He wiped sweat away from his eyes with his sleeve.

Mrs. Throckmorton said, "Don't do that. You'll stain your shirt sleeve." She turned to Slocum. "Would you accept a small cup of apple cider, sir? It's not much, but it is all we can offer."

"Thank you, ma'am," Slocum said, settling down to examine Throckmorton's work. Although he wasn't doing a good job, it was adequate. Slocum told him so.

"Thank you, Mr. Slocum." Throckmorton took a second cup of the cider from his wife. She glared at him, as if disapproving of his gluttony in accepting the cider at all.

"Everything all right now? I see you got the bearings cleaned and greased."

They talked idly. Slocum brought the conversation around to the topic of Cole Mason and his daughter.

"They seem like right nice people," Throckmorton said.

"Especially the daughter," cut in Mrs. Throckmorton. "She goes out of her way to help others less fortunate. I'd say she is generous to a fault. Why, I saw her give the Johnson woman a small bag of coins."

"The Johnsons?" inquired Slocum.

"The widow Johnson and her three sons," supplied Throckmorton. "Her husband died less than a week on the trail. Terrible accident."

"He was foolish. He should never have tried to lift the wagon by himself. It slipped and he was killed," Mrs. Throckmorton said, a note of self-righteousness in her voice. "Grace Mason has done so much helping them along. I know she feeds the three children from time to time."

"What about the preacher?" asked Slocum. The more he found out about Grace, the more she surprised him.

"He's a decent enough sort. I don't hold with his preachings, but that's a personal matter," Mrs. Throckmorton said. "I was raised in a different church with different ways."

"Does he ever mention . . . thieving?" Slocum didn't know quite how to approach the subject. To come right out and ask the Throckmortons if Cole Mason was obviously a bank robber didn't seem right. He kept wondering why he cared. His curiosity had been satisfied when he saw Mason in the clearing.

Yet Slocum hadn't gotten a good look at the man. And Mason had had the chance to gun him down and hadn't taken it. He felt the need to figure out what made the outlaw tick. He had never heard of anyone pretending to be a preacher and then riding out to rob banks. It didn't make good sense. The disguise might fool people for a spell, but when they found out, they'd be even angrier at being duped. People didn't take kindly to putting their trust in a man of the cloth and finding out he was a thief.

"I'd say he was one of the finest men on this wagon train. Certainly the Reverend Mason is a better man than the wagonmaster." Mrs. Throckmorton lowered her voice and rested her hands on her bulging belly. "I've actually seen Mr. August *drinking* hard liquor!"

Slocum clucked his tongue and allowed as to how that was a true evil. Jethro hadn't fooled Mrs. Throckmorton. How many others knew of his occasional sips from the hip flask? Most, he guessed. But he was amazed that Cole Mason didn't seem to drink. He put bank robbing and hard drinking in the same basket. Slocum couldn't imagine Brighton, Villalobos, or Dantley being teetotalers. Hell, he couldn't imagine robbing a bank and not taking a drink afterward to celebrate. He had done it enough times himself to think that everyone else did it, too.

Slocum finished the cider and thanked the Throckmortons. He went off, thinking hard. Something worried him. Instead of finding Jethro and reporting as he'd intended, Slocum mounted his sorrel and started to circle, looking for spoor left by the preacher. The man couldn't have beaten him back to camp by much—certainly not more than half an hour.

Slocum had ridden for less than five minutes when he heard a moaning and groaning that sounded like a distressed steam locomotive struggling uphill.

"Shit," he muttered when he saw Pisser Wingate. The bounty hunter rode his swayback horse holding his head as he rode. The man seemed unkillable.

Slocum loosed the Colt Navy in its holster and prepared to go after the bounty hunter once more.

"Where am I?" called Wingate. "Am I anywhere near a wagon train?"

Slocum's green eyes narrowed. "You looking for someone in particular?" he asked, waiting for Wingate to recognize him. The bounty hunter's eyes were unfocused, and he wobbled.

"Looking for William Deutsch. The son of a bitch is around here someplace. I can smell him."

All Slocum could smell was the man's unwashed odor. He rested his hand on the ebony grips of his Colt.

"Don't know him. Haven't seen any wagon train in these parts, either. You all right?" he asked, riding closer. He didn't think Wingate was trying to trick him. That wasn't the bounty hunter's style.

The side of the man's head had been cut open by the horse's hoof. Slocum had seen men lose their memories after such a head wound. He wondered if this had happened to Wingate.

He had also seen the memory return unexpectedly. He kept his hand on his pistol.

"Do I know you?" Wingate asked, squinting. "I can't recollect much of what's happened over the last few days. Reckon my damned horse threw me." He rubbed the side of his head and winced.

As he moved, his torn buckskins opened along his chest. Slocum almost laughed when he saw a metal plate hidden under the leather. This was why Pisser Wingate seemed invincible. He wore armor under his buckskins. Only a man as strong as Wingate could move normally carrying such weight. Slocum had bounced his slugs off a metal plate. The single cut he had gotten in on the man's side had been between the front and back plates.

Looking closer, he saw curved plates on Wingate's thighs, too. That explained why point-blank firing into the man's leg hadn't bothered him unduly. All the bounty hunter had to do was withstand the impact; the bullet would ricochet off.

"Don't know him," Slocum repeated. He didn't bother answering the man's question. If Wingate had remembered him, he wouldn't have been talking. "But I heard tell of a wagon train about twenty miles to the west of here, coming up from Texas. That's the one you want. I'd bet on it."

"No others?" asked Wingate, obviously confused.

"None," Slocum said with as much assurance as he could muster.

"Twenty miles west?"

Slocum nodded, not trusting himself to say more. Wingate glowered and turned his struggling horse westward. He rode off without another word to Slocum.

Only after the bounty hunter vanished did Slocum let out the pent-up breath threatening to burst his lungs. The bounty hunter seemed to be a force of nature, impervious to every danger. Slocum didn't believe Wingate would ride forever, but he could hope.

By the time the bounty hunter's memory returned, Slocum hoped to be far away—and have a better idea about Cole Mason.

9

John Slocum turned toward the wagon train, all thought of backtracking Cole Mason's trail gone. He had a job to do. He owed Jethro August a report on all he had discovered. His friend had offered good money for very little work, and Slocum had begun feeling twinges of guilt about taking the gold and letting the job fall victim to his curiosity about Mason.

He reined in when he saw Jethro sitting under the same tree he had left him under four days earlier. Slocum dismounted and tethered his sorrel.

"You're back," Jethro said. "I heard rumors passing through the train. Mrs. Throckmorton said you'd been questioning her about all manner of wild-ass things. Don't go shakin' that lady's tree unless you want a peck of trouble, John. She's one bitchy woman. Mark my words. Stay away from the ones about ready to foal. They turn crazy-mean. It's got something to do with protectin' their unborn young'un."

"She certainly disapproves of your drinking and doesn't care who she tells about it," Slocum said, taking the bottle Jethro offered. He downed a swig of the powerful liquor. It burned lips and tongue but left his gullet untouched this time.

"I got troubles, John."

"There are a dozen places the wagon train can ford the river getting into Fort Gibson and then get on into Broken Arrow." Slocum told his friend. He started to sketch them in the dirt, but Jethro wasn't paying attention. "What's wrong?" Slocum asked. "You wanted to keep moving so you'd get a completion bonus. You've holed up here the entire time I was gone."

"The damned cavalry captain came down hard on me, claiming I was aidin' and abettin' a fugitive."

"Did Wingate put the bug in Hawkins's ear?"

"You've come across the young snot? I worried you might. Hawkins seems to be everywhere all the time. Don't know how the man does it."

"He told you not to come into Fort Gibson?"

"Ordered us to stay put until he got to the bottom of this bank robbin' matter. He's takin' it right personal having his town bank robbed under his nose. Damn it, why did Dantley, Brighton, and Villalobos have to do this to me? They could have run in some other direction. Villalobos knows Texas and Mexico. They could have run down there and never cast their damned shadow on me again."

"I suspect they had their reasons," Slocum said. He ought to tell Jethro about the preacher and his involvement with the three robbers, but he didn't.

"If it was just them, I wouldn't mind so much. But Captain Hawkins mentioned that bounty hunter."

"Pisser Wingate," supplied Slocum.

"He's the one. A mean son of a bitch, from all accounts. We should have buried him somewhere." Jethro looked at Slocum. "I wish you had. I truly do, John. His kind don't run off."

"I found out." Slocum related his run-ins with the smelly mountain of a man. Jethro August just shook his head and drank faster. "He's on a wild goose chase," Slocum concluded. "It'll be days before he finds there isn't any wagon train to the west and comes back. He might never get his memory back."

"If he does, you'd better watch your back, John. Hell, we'd all better do that." Jethro looked pained. "He *skinned* Brighton alive?" The wagonmaster shuddered and finished his bottle.

"What are you going to do?" asked Slocum.

"Ain't much I can do but stay put. Less than a week away from Broken Arrow with these tenderfoots and we can't get there. I tell you, John, I feel the bonus money fading. It's evaporating like morning dew on the grass. I'm gonna end up poor and broke and without a cent to my name."

Slocum almost laughed at his friend. He slapped Jethro on the back. "I'll see what can be done. Wingate is gone for the time being. I think I can take care of some of the unpleasantness brewing here in the wagon train."

"What's that?" Jethro August perked up, suddenly alert. "What trouble's this?"

"Don't worry your head over it." Slocum wasn't going to accuse Cole Mason of anything in front of the wagonmaster. He *knew* the man had been the mastermind guiding Dantley and the others and that he was the William Deutsch the bounty hunter sought. But he saw no reason to involve Jethro if the preacher would quietly take his wagon from the train and leave. That might put an end to all their troubles.

Slocum frowned as he thought about Mason doing this. Grace would go with her father. What would he do? Follow them? Slocum didn't have an answer for this, either. There were too many questions lacking decent answers.

Most of all Slocum wasn't sure exactly how he felt about Grace Mason.

He heaved himself to his feet and went off to find the preacher.

The man was sitting in the sun reading his Bible. He scowled when Slocum walked up. After their last conversation just a while back, Slocum didn't blame him much. It had to be upsetting to him even hearing the name Dantley.

"What can I do for you, Mr. Slocum? I'm busy preparing my Sunday sermon."

"This won't take long, Deutsch." Slocum watched the preacher's expression cloud over. Anger flashed and faded as fast as it had appeared. Resignation settled over the man like a heavy woolen blanket.

"You know. I was afraid someone would find out one day."

"Pisser Wingate did."

"You keep mentioning him. I haven't seen hide nor hair of him for almost a year."

At this bald-faced lie Slocum blinked. "Wingate came to the wagon train looking for you. Of course you've seen him. You were there when he killed Villalobos and Brighton."

"Sir?"

The expression on Mason's face confused Slocum. If he hadn't known better, he would have thought the preacher knew nothing of the men's deaths.

"Villalobos was gutted and Brighton skinned alive. You

were there. I saw you there. You had the chance to use your scattergun on me and didn't. For that I thank you."

"Sir, I do *not* know what you mean. I admit to being William Deutsch—at one time. Those days are long past. I haven't even thought of robbing a bank since I took up God's work almost twelve years ago. When Grace's mother died, I realized I could not leave her alone in the world. She was only eight and did not know my sordid history. I have spread the word of God, not lawlessness. Those days still haunt me, though."

"Why is Wingate so eager to take your scalp?"

Cole Mason heaved a deep sigh and closed his Bible. "The man used to be a sheriff up in Dakota Territory. I robbed the bank—I can't even remember the name of the town now, it has been so long. Wingate lost not only his life's savings in the robbery, but the townspeople also blamed him and fired him from his job."

"He's been holding a grudge for a powerful long time," observed Slocum. "There must be more to it than losing money and a job."

"You force me to confess to crimes that revolt me," said Mason. "In the robbery, a man was killed. I have reason to believe it was Wingate's brother."

"You killed his brother? Why isn't there a murder warrant out for you?"

"You misunderstand. Wingate's brother was killed during the robbery—by Wingate. He fired at me as I rode off. A stray shot hit his brother, killing him instantly, I was told later."

Slocum considered this. Much of Pisser Wingate's mindless determination in tracking down Mason was explained. It certainly took away a large measure of the big man's guilt over killing his own brother.

Mason laid his hand on the Bible and said in a solemn

voice. "There is no reason for you to believe this, Mr. Slocum, but as God is my witness, I have not robbed anyone in the past twelve years. Wingate might be my nemesis, but the only crime for which I claim any guilt since then is that of pride."

"What?"

"I am inordinately proud of my daughter and my righteousness over the years. What I have done to inspire Wingate's towering wrath is long dead."

Slocum didn't know whether to believe the preacher or think him the best liar in the world.

"A moment, sir. Do not get upset at what I am about to show you." Mason disappeared into the wagon and came out with a pistol case. Slocum tensed, his hand twitching slightly. Mason's calmness kept him from pulling his Colt.

"This is the Remington Dragoon I used during my lawless days. As you can see, it has not been out of its case in all that time."

Slocum took the pistol from the case. The old blackpowder pistol weighed heavy in his hand. He hefted it and frowned. "It's been oiled," he said, running his finger along the blued barrel. "Recently."

"I do penance," said Mason. "I test myself by taking it out and seeing if any of the primitive urges that once drove me to a life of crime remain."

"Do they?"

Cole Mason smiled sadly. "At times I feel the pull. How well I resist depends on my faith in God. My faith is very strong, Mr. Slocum. I have not backslid."

Slocum considered this. He had seen Mason with the outlaws—or he thought he had. The size was about the same, and the man had worn the red bandanna he'd seen inside Mason's wagon. Slocum had to admit, though, that he had never seen the bank robbers' face clearly. The hat brim had always shielded the eyes, and the bandanna had masked the face. Still, Slocum wondered. The inexplicable reluctance of the outlaw leader to cut him down when he had the chance went along with Mason's professed religious faith.

"Captain Hawkins up in Fort Gibson is likely to know about you," Slocum finally said. "Wingate rummaged through their posters until he found yours in their back files."

"He wanted to be sure the authorities knew I was a criminal," Mason said. "I should pay for my sins, but it is so difficult."

"A man shouldn't pay for something that far in the past," Slocum said.

"A sin blackens the soul forever," Mason said piously, hand on the Bible.

"I'm sure it does," Slocum said, thinking more about what the effect of Hawkins arresting the man would be on Grace than on her father. If Mason was telling the truth, it wasn't right for him to be locked up for crimes that counted as history.

If a debt had to be paid, Brighton and Villalobos had already given more than the law required.

"Wingate might be around, if he ever gets his memory back. I got rid of him for a spell, but he's a wily son of a bitch."

"His persistence could have been put to better use. You cannot know how uneasy I have been over the years knowing that a man like him has dogged my steps. I barely avoided him a year ago. Prior to that, he has appeared at irregular intervals to bedevil me."

"I can guess," Slocum allowed, remembering his fights with the bounty hunter. The man was a juggernaut, never stopping, always coming with more muscle and determination and downright meanness than any human ought to possess.

"This had to happen someday," said the preacher, venting a gusty sigh. "I hope you will not tell Grace. She is ignorant of my sordid background."

"There's no reason to tell her," said Slocum, glad that this matter had resolved itself. "If I get to Captain Hawkins's wanted posters, I might be able to slip yours from the stack. No one in Fort Gibson would think twice about a new preacher man being a former bank robber."

"I cannot let you do this for me. You'd endanger yourself needlessly."

"What danger is that?" asked Slocum. "The only problem I see is Pisser Wingate. He knows the poster exists— and the adjutant wouldn't let him take it."

"We can be long gone before the bounty hunter returns," Mason said reluctantly. "I hate to run. I'd my heart set on settling down and establishing a decent ministry in Broken Arrow."

"I'll get rid of the poster. We can see where this takes us. Captain Hawkins is likely to chase off Wingate if he gets too obnoxious. You look after Grace until I get back."

The preacher started to ask Slocum what he meant, then clamped his mouth shut.

Slocum passed through the camp, checked on the Throckmorton wagon, and saw that the wheels had been adequately repaired. Others in the wagon train were milling about, grumbling at the delay. Slocum saw that Jethro had to tell them soon what was holding up their progress or they would pull out on their own. All chance at a bonus would evaporate then, and the cavalry captain would have Jethro's scalp for disobeying a direct order.

"Where you headed, John?" Jethro called, seeing his friend mounting his horse.

"Got to ride back into Fort Gibson. I'll see if I can't persuade Captain Hawkins to lift the travel ban. There's no good reason to keep everyone from getting to all that land."

"This doesn't have anything to do with Wingate, does it? That man's bad medicine, I tell you."

"Doesn't much matter if it does, Jethro. Go tell the people in the train not to be so antsy. We'll be moving again in a day or so or know the reason."

"Be careful," Jethro called. The portly wagonmaster frowned mightily and went to talk with the more anxious settlers.

Slocum rode slowly, wondering how to approach the young cavalry captain with his handful of requests. Grace wanted him to talk with Dantley and give him a message —but the preacher had said Dantley was no kin. Slocum allowed as to how that might be an embarrassing topic for the man. His background wasn't the most upright and law-abiding, but Slocum had also heard a ring of sincerity and truth in Mason's voice when he said he hadn't robbed any banks for twelve years.

Slocum scratched his head. Too many unanswered questions were popping up and making him crazy with burning curiosity. He decided to tackle them one by one. First off had to be solving Jethro's problem with the cavalry officer.

The rest might fall into place, given enough time.

Or so Slocum thought until he heard the sharp crack of a rifle. The bullet's impact on the side of his head knocked him from the sorrel. Unmoving, he lay in the dusty Oklahoma road.

10

Bees buzzed inside Slocum's head. He stirred and tried to roll onto his back, but instinct caused him to lie flat on his belly and play dead. Whoever had bushwhacked him might still be watching.

Possibilities ran through his aching head. Cole Mason? What reason did the preacher have to back-shoot him if he thought things were working out? That this was the action of a road agent never entered Slocum's thoughts.

It had to be Pisser Wingate's doing. Nothing else made any sense. A thin trickle of blood oozed down his cheek and dripped into the powdery dust as he struggled to get his senses back. Looking out through one blurred eye told him he had a ways to go. But one sense alerted him before the others.

Ringing in his ears kept him from hearing. His vision remained blurred. But his nose twitched when he caught Wingate's distinctively bad odor.

"Gotcha this time, boy," he heard the bounty hunter say, as if from a hundred miles away. "Nobody jerks me off the way you did and gets by with it."

Slocum tried not to tense when he heard a carbine lever cocking and a new cartridge sliding into a firing chamber. He could never spin around, find his Colt Navy, and get it firing accurately in time to save his life.

"I got better uses for my ammo than plugging lifeless bodies," Wingate said. "Send me on a wild goose chase, will you. Harumph."

Slocum chanced a look as Wingate rode off, his sway-backed horse bowlegged under its huge load. A long-barreled, large-caliber rifle rested over Wingate's shoulder. Slocum cursed his own foolishness. He should never have thought the bounty hunter would never use a firearm after hearing Cole Mason's story. Wingate *enjoyed* carving men with a knife. That didn't mean he didn't also like drygulching them with a rifle or pistol.

Slocum decided to play it safe and simply lie in the dirt for a few more minutes.

A wet nose nuzzling his face brought him fully awake. To his surprise, the sun hung an hour lower in the sky. He hadn't played dead; he had passed out. Reaching up, he pushed his sorrel's muzzle away and patted the horse.

"You're still looking after me, aren't you?" The horse whinnied and tried to push him back to the ground. "It's no time to play, old girl." He flung his arms around the horse's neck and let the powerful animal help him to his feet. He steadied himself for a few seconds until a bout of dizziness passed.

Strength came back faster as he walked beside his horse. In a few minutes, he tried mounting. His legs turned to butter, then steadied. Slocum pulled himself into his saddle and felt better than he had since being shot. He touched the spot on the side of his head. A dull, annoying ache filled his skull, but it was better than having his head blown off.

He considered returning to the wagon train and immediately discarded that notion. Pisser Wingate had recovered his memory faster than Slocum had hoped. The bounty hunter couldn't be allowed to drygulch at will without paying the price for it.

Slocum checked his Winchester and the Colt hanging at his left side and decided he was up to tracking the bounty hunter. Payment had to be extracted or Wingate would keep on until more people died.

"I hope his head feels as bad as mine," he said aloud. The horse turned and stared at him. "You should have kicked him harder," Slocum said. "Not that it matters. He's got a head harder than rock." He wished he had, too.

Slocum bent low, holding the horse's neck as he studied the dry road. The dust didn't hold hoof-prints well, but Wingate had strayed from the road and onto the grassy shoulder. The weight he put on his horse caused distinctive imprints that Slocum tracked without much difficulty. When he saw in which direction the bounty hunter was headed, Slocum cursed long and loud.

"The son of a bitch is so single-minded, it makes me wonder why he doesn't choke on his own bile."

Wingate was riding directly to the wagon train.

Slocum picked up the pace and saw that Wingate wasn't going straight in, as he'd first thought. If he had, he'd've been at the preacher's wagon a long time back. For whatever reason, the bounty hunter skirted the encampment and kept to the thickly wooded area to the south.

Slocum considered telling Jethro August and getting some of the others in the train to help in keeping Wingate at bay. He decided surprise counted for more than numbers. Wingate had no sense of fear. Hatred and guilt drove the man, not good sense.

"John?" came a soft query.

He swung about, his Colt coming free of the soft leather holster. He had it aimed and cocked before he realized it was Grace Mason who had called his name.

"You surely are jumpy today," she said. "I saw you speaking with Papa and decided not to interrupt. But you rushed off before I could say anything to you. You're not trying to avoid me, are you?"

"Where's your pa?" Slocum asked. The preacher would draw the bounty hunter like flies to shit.

"You sound as if you're more interested in him and his soul-saving than you are in me . . . and my pleasing ways." Grace smiled coquettishly and thrust out her chest. Her breasts strained against her blouse.

Slocum had no time for this. His head hurt, and an anger burned like fire inside. Wingate had to be stopped. He had no time for dalliance with the preacher's daughter.

"This is life and death," he said. "For your father. Wingate came back sooner than I'd've thought possible."

"So? What does he have to do with Papa?"

"There's no time to explain. Get on back to your wagon. No, wait." Slocum knew he still wasn't thinking clearly because of the head wound. He couldn't send her back to her father. Danger would whirl there like the center of a tornado. "Find Jethro and tell him Wingate is back. He'll know what to do."

"What about you, John? You . . . you're hurt! I see blood on your face. Let me tend your—"

"No! Get the hell back. I don't know what you were doing out here, but it's dangerous."

"John, really. This is . . ." The woman bit off her words when she saw the set of his face. "I'm sorry. This is important, isn't it?" Without another word, she spun and hurried off in the direction of Jethro's campsite.

Slocum watched her go, a lump in his throat. She was one handsome woman. He had to keep telling himself he was hunting down Wingate for his own reasons, not to spare her from learning of her father's bank robbing career.

Slocum turned cold inside when he thought of the reward on his own head. If Wingate had searched the Fort Gibson files thoroughly, he could have found a poster on John Slocum, judge killer. Slocum told himself he was hunting down Pisser Wingate as much for his own benefit as for any coming Cole Mason's way.

He started tracking in earnest. The spoor wasn't difficult to follow. Wingate made no attempt to hide his trail because he had no reason to believe anyone was following him. Slocum moved through the stand of pines as silent as a ghost. He spotted Wingate setting up the long-barreled rifle on a firing tripod. The bounty hunter might have been getting ready to slaughter buffalo.

Slocum remembered the metal sheets Wingate wore on his body and legs. Shooting the huge man there would stagger him, but the dead-on-target bullet wouldn't do much else. It had to be a head shot or nothing.

He had been the best sniper in the Confederacy, but Slocum knew he couldn't make this shot with any confidence. The light shifted and put Wingate in shadow. The thick trees hindered a direct shot, too. He had to get closer and be sure.

Wingate hummed to himself, the happiest the bounty hunter had ever seemed. He moved around and squatted behind his rifle, sighting along his long barrel.

Slocum nodded. The man worked well. He had been a fool to think the bounty hunter had forsaken firearms after accidentally killing his own brother. Wingate was as good with a rifle as he was with his huge bowie knife.

Slocum would be better.

Dismounting, Slocum circled and came up on Wingate from behind. The man's entire attention was focused on the sodbusters' encampment and Cole Mason's wagon. Wingate had seen that bushwhacking worked well. He must figure that if he killed Mason, no one would object if he took the body back to claim the reward.

Or maybe he didn't care squat about the reward. He might want Mason dead to soothe his own guilt feelings over his brother.

Slocum pulled his Winchester from its scabbard and levered a shell into the chamber. Wingate jerked upright, alert. The man had the senses of a wild animal.

"You're a dead man if you move a muscle, Wingate," Slocum called. Even as he spoke, he knew the bounty hunter wasn't the surrendering kind. His finger came back on the trigger before the last word left his lips. Even then, he missed Wingate.

His bullet ripped into a tree and sent sap and splinters flying. All he had accomplished was to warn Wingate—and separate the man from his rifle. Wingate had hit and rolled, diving into the dense thicket. His rifle and tripod remained behind.

Slocum listened intently. All he heard were stirrings from the wagon train, as the settlers wondered what the ruckus was. Mrs. Throckmorton's voice carried above all the others as she loudly demanded that Jethro do something.

Cautiously advancing, Slocum checked the rifle Wingate had dropped. He worked for a few seconds and jammed the mechanism. One lesson he had learned painfully was never to leave a working weapon behind. Too often its owner came back for it—and used it.

Slocum followed the bounty hunter into the thicket. He found bits of buckskin on the thorny bushes. When he found a particularly long one, Slocum slowed and listened intently. Pisser Wingate hadn't fled *that* fast. Slocum thought he might be laying a trap for the unwary. He heard and saw nothing, but his nose picked up the familiar stench.

Almost too late, Slocum stepped back and lifted the muzzle of his rifle. Wingate had climbed a tree and waited on the overhanging branch, knife in hand. Slocum fired at the same instant Wingate jumped.

A bull-throated roar filled the woods. Slocum knew his bullet had hit the man squarely in the belly. He also knew the man's huge bulk carried him to the ground, knocking the wind from his lungs.

"You're dead," Wingate said, looming over him like an elemental force. The expression on the bounty hunter's face showed confusion and not a little fear. He was so sure of himself and his marksmanship he could never believe Slocum hadn't died on the road.

"I came back," Slocum growled. "For you!" He heaved and caught Wingate off balance. Toppling to the side, Wingate presented a perfect target for Slocum.

His Colt slid easily into his hand. Where his rifle had gone, he didn't know or care. For close-in fighting, the six-shooter was better. Slocum fired pointblank five times. Three times he heard the bullets strike metal. The other two times brought groans from Wingate and small geysers of blood.

The bounty hunter lurched away and rushed into the forest. Slocum used his last round. He heard it strike the hidden metal armor Wingate wore. His only consolation was the way Wingate staggered and fell. Slocum rolled and came to his feet, finding his rifle.

A moment's dizziness assailed him, but it passed. He shoved his Colt into his holster and ran after Wingate to finish him off. Even a vicious animal deserved to be put out of its misery after it had been wounded in a hunt.

Slocum knew his prey had gotten away when he heard the pounding of a horse's hooves. Swerving, he headed for his sorrel. Wingate wasn't going to get away this time.

"Catch 'em, old girl. You can do it. You're rested, and his horse is carrying quite a load." Slocum patted his horse. They took off with a lurch. He thought it would be an easy task overtaking the fleeing bounty hunter, but he was wrong.

The sun hung low in the west, and they reached the banks of the Arkansas River before Slocum caught sight of Wingate. The man's horse had stepped in a prairie dog hold and broken a leg. Wingate bellowed in rage and took off for a rocky cliff, leaving his suffering horse behind. Slocum rode up and stared at the wide-eyed, frightened beast. He did what Wingate should have. Slocum was sorry to see such a valiant animal die.

Killing Wingate would be that much easier. A man should tend to his own horse and not leave the chore for someone else, no matter what.

"Running scared, Wingate?" he called. Slocum didn't expect a reply. He just hoped for some sign of where the man had run to. He got it in a tiny cascade of rocks down a steep slope.

Slocum rode over and stared down the embankment. Wingate scurried like a rat, favoring his right side. Slocum knew that neither of the wounds he had inflicted were serious, but they slowed the bounty hunter a mite. He unlimbered his Winchester and sighted, getting off a good shot. He brought the man down but didn't kill him. He waited several minutes for another shot at Wingate.

When it didn't come, Slocum dismounted and started down the steep slope. He expected an attack—and it came with the fury of an Oklahoma tornado.

"I'll learn you to fool with me, boy!" Pisser Wingate erupted from behind a boulder.

Slocum swung the butt of his Winchester around and caught Wingate under the chin. The man's head snapped back, and he stumbled and fell. Slocum knew then that the wounds he had inflicted were weakening this mountain of a man. He showed him no mercy. He swung his rifle around and aimed and fired in a smooth motion.

Slocum cursed when he heard the heavy rifle slug careen off Wingate's body armor. The impact had to hurt, but he would have preferred the lead slug to go through the bounty hunter's immense body.

"Kill you," growled Wingate. He stumbled to his feet. Form the depths of his fringed buckskins he whipped out his bowie knife and attacked.

Slocum had faced death before, but Wingate's mindless attack still caught him off guard. He fired and missed. Then he found himself surrounded by powerful arms and heavy stench.

The gravel under his feet gave way, and Slocum turned to one side. This might have been his end. Instead, it gave him the chance to push Wingate past and use the rifle's barrel on the back of the man's head. Wingate fell to hands and knees, losing his knife.

Before Slocum could recover, Wingate circled his legs and pulled him down. Slocum crashed hard onto his back. His head felt as if it had turned into a rotted melon about ready to split. The world spun in wild circles, and his gut churned. Vomit rose and caught in his throat.

"You're buzzard bait now, boy," Wingate declared. "I'm gonna do you good."

Slocum kicked out blindly and caught Wingate on the knee. The bounty hunter grunted and went down, hands still clutching for Slocum. More unconscious than aware, Slocum fought to get away from the still-powerful man. He barely got to the edge of a butte. Twenty feet below, the Arkansas River boiled and churned with the fury of spring runoff water.

Like a grizzly, Pisser Wingate rose up above Slocum. And like a majestic tree chopped down, he toppled into the river when Slocum fired the rifle still clutched in his hand.

Slocum sagged for an instant, then got to his hands and knees and looked over the verge into the foaming green, white-flecked river. Wingate tried to swim.

"Help me. The metal . . ."

Those were the bounty hunter's last words before his head vanished under the water.

Slocum sat and stared for long minutes. Pisser Wingate didn't surface. The metal armor that had saved him repeatedly had finally meant his death.

John Slocum felt no sense of accomplishment or relief. All had been drained from him. What remained was a head that threatened to explode and a body that had been pushed beyond the limits of his endurance.

11

Slocum blanked out repeatedly as he made his way along the shale slope and back to his sorrel. The fight with Wingate had caused the head wound to act up something fierce. He wanted to shout in pain by the time he climbed into the saddle.

"How far can I go?" he asked the horse. Neither the sorrel nor he had any good idea how long he could ride in this condition. He hadn't been seriously wounded by the bounty hunter—this time. But his head wound when Wingate bushwhacked him was another matter. Slocum fought to keep his balance, teetering gracelessly in the saddle as he rode.

That Pisser Wingate had drowned was small consolation. He couldn't keep a coherent thought running for longer than a few seconds, but one recurred over and over: find a doctor. He was feverish, and the Oklahoma spring countryside refused to stop spinning in crazy, ever-widening circles.

"Find me a town," he told the sorrel. Then he gave the horse her head. The next thing he remembered clearly were two small boys yelling and running around. One jumped up and grabbed his horse's reins. He did what he could to keep the animal from rearing. Then he fought to keep from falling out of the saddle.

"Needs help bad. Get Doc Cliett. Get him, get him quick!"

Slocum felt strong hands gripping him. He fought weakly before succumbing. Wooden steps creaked under him, and he smelled a saloon and heard loud voices turn mute.

Through the silence came one stentorian bellow, "Don't go bringing in anybody that's gonna die in my saloon. I won't stand for it!"

"Nobody's ever gonna accuse you of having a heart of gold, Thom. So shut up, will you? He ain't gonna die, not unless the doc's drunk on your rotgut whiskey again."

"He's on the wagon," grumbled the saloon owner. Slocum looked up and a huge man filled his field of vision. For a heart-stopping instant he thought Wingate had come back to life. He didn't smell the bounty hunter's all too familiar stench, though. The only odors coming to him were stale beer and cheap cologne.

"Who?" he croaked.

"Maybe he wants to start a tab, Thom. Will you give him credit? You can get him to sign over everything he owns before he knows what he's doing."

"Hell, he ain't an Injun," Thom said.

"Did you ever collect off Danny Tenkiller?" asked another.

Slocum's attention faded as the room began to spin

again. He heard heavy boot steps approaching, then felt a cool hand on his forehead.

"Get him into the back room. I don't want you jackasses bouncing him around getting him up the stairs to my office till I've looked him over good and proper."

"Dr. Cliett?" Slocum got out.

"He knows you, Doc. And he still came here. Glory be, this must be a miracle."

"Get him into the back room," the doctor ordered. Slocum knew they were carrying him, but he might have been drifting on a white, puffy springtime cloud.

The next few hours passed by in snippets of overheard conversation. He knew he had slept when he awoke with a start. His hand flashed to his head. He winced as pain jolted him.

"Stay flat on your damned back," Doc Cliett ordered. "Somebody's shot up your head and given you a concussion."

"What's that mean?" Slocum asked.

"You should take it easy for a few days. How long since that head wound, young fella?"

"Happened this morning."

"You're lucky to be alive. If you'd passed out where people couldn't find you, you might have gone into a coma and died."

"Lucky to be alive," Slocum repeated, thinking of his fight with Pisser Wingate.

"Damned right. And for my services, I'm not going to charge you but ten dollars in gold." As Slocum reached for his shirt pocket, the doctor said. "Don't fret none. I already took it. You've got a fair amount of coin jingling in your pockets. Reckon the sheriff might want to know what brings a gunshot fellow like you through Tahlequah."

"Tahlequah? That's where I am?"

"About ten miles outside Fort Gibson, if that means anything to you."

"It does. I know Captain Hawkins."

"Makes life easier all around, you knowing the garrison commander. You wouldn't mind if the sheriff contacts Hawkins?"

"I'd appreciate it if he would. I was on my way up there to talk with a prisoner of his when I was drygulched."

"You don't look like a lawman." The doctor lounged in a straight-backed chair, his boots hiked up to a box filled with whiskey from St. Louis.

Slocum recovered slowly, knowing the doctor was pumping him for information he wouldn't likely give if he had his full senses about him.

Shaking his head made it feel as if something was rattling loose inside.

"Here. I prescribe a shot of Thom's best." Doc Cliett handed over an unopened bottle of Kentucky whiskey—or so the label read. Slocum smiled when he realized he was able to read without the words blurring. Even better, he knew the whiskey hadn't been within five hundred miles of bluegrass. "You're not drinking?" Slocum asked.

"Decided a few months back to become a teetotaler." Cliett let out a belch and rubbed his loudly grumbling belly. "Bad things happening down here."

"I'm with Jethro August's wagon train," Slocum said.

"August? Never heard of him, but then there's not many of these wagonmasters I've heard of these days. Things are going from bad to worse. There's talk about opening up Indian land to settlers. Not a good idea taking their land away. The Indians, I mean."

"We ran afoul of a Choctaw raiding party about a week back," Slocum said, slowly pulling himself to a sitting position. His head settled down, and a moment of dizziness

SLOCUM AND THE PREACHER'S DAUGHTER   111

passed quickly. He took a long pull on the whiskey. The buzzing in his ears vanished, replaced by a familiar burning in his stomach.

"Powerful whiskey," observed Doc Cliett. "For you, it's the best remedy I can find in Tahlequah."

"I can ride on out?"

"Can't stop you. There's no need to stop you, either. You going on up to Fort Gibson?"

"That's where I was headed. Captain Hawkins has stopped the wagon train while he investigates a robbery."

"You and this prisoner you're going to visit any kin?"

Slocum snorted. He knew better than to shake his head now. "Hardly. Dantley used to work for Jethro August."

"That's why the eager captain stopped the wagon train, eh?"

"I'm trying to grease the tracks and get the wagons rolling again. If Dantley will tell Captain Hawkins that neither August nor anyone else in the wagon train had anything to do with the robberies, that might satisfy him."

"We can always use new settlers in these parts, I reckon," Doc Cliett said. "Gives me more patients. I can use the money."

Slocum looked at the doctor, who smiled crookedly. "Gave up drinking, but the gambling spirit hits me real often." Cliett took the bottle from Slocum and put it on a crate. "You get on out of here. I haven't killed you, and there's nothing more I can do to you to get a bigger fee."

"Much obliged," Slocum said, standing. There was another moment of dizziness, but then he felt better than he had since being bushwhacked.

Together with the doctor he left the back room and went to the front of the saloon. Halfway to the swinging doors, they heard gunshots.

"What in tarnation can that be?" grumbled the doctor.

He hurried to the doors and peered over the ornate tops.

Slocum pushed past and stood on the edge of the wood planking. He looked up and down the street and saw nothing unusual. Across the street a Cherokee came out of the general store to imitate Slocum's curiosity. Two other men poked their heads out of a dry goods store next to the saloon.

A third shot brought Slocum around to stare in the other direction. It took him a few seconds to figure out the letters on the window and determine that the glass-fronted structure was the Tahlequah bank. Inside he saw figures moving—and most had their hands stuck up high in the air.

"Looks like the bank's being robbed," Doc Cliett said in disgust. "Best go find the sheriff and get him on this. That lazy old codger'll never do anything on his own." The doctor hurried off past the bank and down the street. Slocum just stood and watched. He had caught a flash of red through the large window. He had a good idea who was sticking up the bank.

"You got to hand it to him," Slocum said to himself when he saw the robber burst out the bank's front door. "He's audacious."

Red bandanna pulled up over his nose, battered brown hat brim down, and the long tan canvas duster flapping around his ankles, the robber exploded from the bank and vaulted into the saddle. He wheeled around, then paused when he saw Slocum watching.

For a long moment, neither moved. Then the robber lifted the long barrel of the Remington in his hand and touched the brim of his hat with it in mock salute. Then he put heels to the flanks of his horse and raced off in a cloud of dust.

Slocum turned and watched the robber vanish down the Tahlequah street. A few seconds later, he thought someone had poured hot water down an anthill. The bank customers boiled out shouting and carrying on. A clerk trailed them and bellowed, "Robbery! Get the sheriff! The bank's been robbed!"

Doc Cliett and a portly man waddled up from a side street. Slocum perched on a hitching rail and watched the drama unfold. It took the lawman a good five minutes to get everyone settled down and another ten to piece together a lucid story.

"Consarn it!" he finally called. "Why'd it take you so dang long to tell me? The damned road agent's miles from here by now!"

"You just didn't want to go traipsin' after nobody who'd shoot at you, Sheriff," accused the teller. "We're trying to wire Captain Hawkins up in Fort Gibson and let him know what's happened. He'll get us some action."

Slocum heard angry grumblings in the gathered crowd about the sheriff's lack of courage and attention to duty. When the Western Union clerk came up, he shook his head.

Slocum sauntered over and stood close enough to hear what was happening.

"Can't explain it," the wire clerk said. "Lines are dead between here and Fort Gibson. They went dead just about fifteen minutes ago, just before the robbery."

"The damned owlhoot cut the wires," the sheriff said. "Fat lot of good your Captain Hawkins is going to do us. I want a posse. Who'll come with me to hunt down the bank robber?"

Three or four men volunteered. Slocum looked at the doctor, who studied him like some kind of specimen he'd just found. Slocum pushed through the crowd and said, "Doc Cliett and I saw everything from the front of the saloon. I saw the robber ride out—down that way." He pointed down the street.

"Who in hell are you?" demanded the sheriff.

"He got bushwhacked. He's with a wagon train down south a ways," supplied the doctor. "It's like he said. We watched the robbery. I went to get you, and he stayed on the stoop."

"You willing to ride along with the posse?" asked the sheriff.

"Be glad to," Slocum said. "I got business in Fort Gibson, but it can wait a spell."

"Get mounted. We're gonna catch ourselves a bank robber!" shouted the rotund sheriff.

Slocum went to his sorrel and gingerly climbed into the saddle. The doctor had fixed him up as good as could be expected. His head still hurt, but his vision had cleared and the ringing had left his ears. More than this, it felt good to be astride his horse again.

He waited for the posse to form. The sheriff pulled up alongside and said, "Show us where the goldarned varmint went. We'll follow you, mister."

Slocum took off at a gallop, then slowed when he reached the edge of Tahlequah. He had recognized Cole Mason from the bandanna and the old black-powder Remington he used—and he knew the robber had recognized him. He had saluted before riding out of town. As much as Slocum admired the man's daring, he felt a bit cheated. He had believed Mason when the preacher told him he hadn't been robbing banks for over twelve years.

Still, Slocum wasn't about to turn the man over to the posse. The sheriff was a decent enough sort, if incompetent. Those with him, though, had blood in their eyes. If they caught the robber, they'd hang him on the spot, and the sheriff wouldn't be able to stop them. Slocum figured

Mason took his chances every time he held up a bank, but he had a grudging admiration for him. When Slocum had engaged in such thievery, he'd always preferred being daring to being cautious.

Even more than the chance Mason might swing from a big oak tree's limb, Slocum didn't want to be the one to tell Grace about her father's death.

"Why are you slowing down?" asked the sheriff.

"There's something odd about the trail. Look, Sheriff. See what I mean?" Slocum dismounted and pointed to the fresh cuts in the grass where a horse had recently run.

"I don't know what you mean."

"Let's see." Two others in the small posse jumped down and examined the ground. Slocum saw they knew more about tracking than the sheriff did, but not as much as Cole Mason. The preacher had planted a false trail leading toward Fort Gibson. A very good tracker would have spotted the ploy—a good one might have been suspicious.

The men with the posse took the bogus trail at face value.

"He went that way, Sheriff!" one cried.

"Looks as if your man is right," Slocum said, nodding sagely. Happy that they were on the elusive outlaw's trail, the others followed like sheep. They rode hard for another few minutes until their horses began to tire quickly.

"Sheriff," Slocum called, "let's pull up and rest. We won't catch anybody running our horses into the ground. And I don't know about yours, but mine can stand a long drink of water."

"Reckon you're right," the sheriff said. Sweat poured down the man's face from the exertion of riding so hard. His own horse's flanks were flecked with lather. If they had run another five minutes, the animal would have collapsed from exhaustion.

"We have to catch the robber before sundown. If we don't have him in sight by then, we're lost," complained a florid man in the posse.

"We're on the right trail," Slocum said, leading his horse to a small stream. He pointed to the muddy banks where an animal had watered recently. He guessed that it had been a small cow, perhaps even a calf that had wandered off from its mother. It might have been a horse. The posse all believed the track belonged to the robber.

Slocum kept them moving until dusk, when it became too difficult to find any tracks, either real or imagined. He slowed and then circled the spot where he had found a few hoofprints. From the very first, he had believed Cole Mason had started toward Fort Gibson, laying the false trail, then circled and returned to the wagon train. Whoever belonged to these tracks had ridden from the north, not the south.

The posse was too tired and disheartened to care.

"Let's get on back to Tahlequah," suggested the sheriff. "We ain't gonna find the outlaw tonight. There's not a good moon to track by for another week."

Slocum glanced up into the pitch-black sky and saw that the sheriff was right on this point. With any luck the preacher had been back by the campfire and had a good hot meal fixed by his daughter. At the thought of Grace Mason, Slocum heaved a deep sigh. He couldn't lie to himself. Much of what he was doing in Cole Mason's behalf was really for Grace's benefit.

"We're not too far from Fort Gibson, are we?" asked Slocum. They had ridden in circles for part of the day until he wasn't absolutely certain where the cavalry stockade lay. "Why don't we ride on into the fort and tell Captain Hawkins what happened?"

"We're returning to town," the sheriff said flatly.

"There's no need to involve the cavalry in our town's private affair."

"I have to go into Fort Gibson anyway," Slocum said. "Wouldn't be any trouble letting the authorities know what's happened." Slocum knew that the Western Union lines might be fixed by now. Mason had clipped the lines running between Tahlequah and Fort Gibson to keep the cavalry away. The break in the line would be easily found and fixed, so he risked nothing by offering to inform Hawkins. The captain probably already knew of the robbery.

"Let him report it to Hawkins. We ain't got nothing to lose by doing that, Sheriff."

"Do it," the portly man said in a tired voice. "Tell Hawkins he can get a full report from me if he stops by."

"That I will, Sheriff," said Slocum. He watched the dispirited posse return to Tahlequah. As they vanished into the darkness, he headed up the road to Fort Gibson, feeling a combination of elation and despair.

Although he was happy that the preacher had eluded the posse, he was saddened that the man had lied to him. The bank robber had been the same man he had encountered in the forest after Villalobos and Brighton were killed—and was the leader Dantley refused to indict. Mason had a way about him, that Slocum couldn't deny.

He just didn't know whether to admire him or be angry about his lies.

12

The road into Fort Gibson was deserted. Slocum rode slowly, making sure he didn't lose his way. Too many side trails left the road for him to be absolutely certain where he was going. Only when the columns of smoke from dozens of evening cooking fires appeared did he feel secure. He homed in on them and soon saw bright lights from saloons and other businesses still open.

He dismounted outside the Wicked Lady Saloon, a powerful thirst settling on him like a dusty blanket. He had been knocked about, bushwhacked, and witness to a robbery—and had gotten rid of Pisser Wingate once and for all. Slocum figured he deserved a small drink to celebrate.

The frosted glass doors stood open. For a few seconds he hesitated, letting his eyes adjust to the bright light inside. Then he went to the bar and ordered a whiskey.

"All we got's trade whiskey," the barkeep said.

Slocum silently pulled a double eagle from his pocket.

He was thankful that Doc Cliett was an honest thief. He had overcharged, but he hadn't robbed him blind. The bartender licked his lips and looked around.

"Maybe we got something better than trade. You want some cognac?"

"I want whiskey that won't gag me," Slocum said. "Where's the boss's special bottle?"

"He'd horsewhip me something fierce if I used his private bottle." The barkeep's eyes widened slightly as Slocum spun the coin on the bar. The distinctive chiming of gold against wood as the coin settled convinced him to take the chance.

A half-filled bottle without any label flashed out from under the bar, was poured, and vanished. Slocum tasted the liquor, then smiled. This *was* good.

"You won't be wanting much more, will you, mister?"

"One more," Slocum said. The two smooth drinks cost him five dollars out of the twenty-dollar gold piece, but he didn't care. The warmth in his belly made him feel whole again. As he turned to look at the others in the saloon, he saw the barkeep pour two shot glasses of water into the bottle.

He smiled. The owner must measure the whiskey to be sure no one raided his private stock.

"Is Captain Hawkins over at the stockade?" he asked the barkeep.

The man shrugged. "Who knows? Ever since he got the bug up his ass about catching the men what upped and robbed the bank a while back, he hasn't put in regular hours."

"He's got one robber," Slocum said. "What about the others?"

"Haven't heard."

With that, the bartender moved to the far end of the bar

and started polishing glasses. Slocum finished his drink and left, satisfied that Hawkins hadn't come across Pisser Wingate's bloody handiwork. That made it easier getting in to see Dantley once more. As long as Captain Hawkins was eager to capture the other outlaws, he'd go to any lengths—even letting Slocum talk to the prisoner.

Slocum went to the stockade and told the guard he wanted to see the captain. The bored sentry motioned him through. Slocum found the garrison commander at work at his desk.

"You again?" Hawkins said, a sour look on his face. "We're not letting the wagon train move until we figure out how Jethro August and the robbers tie in together."

Slocum sighed. "They don't. Jethro hired them. He didn't know they planned to go on a robbing spree using the wagon train as a cover. Even if he's got something to do with your bank robbery, the sodbusters in the train don't. Let them pass through town and get their land deeds squared away over in Broken Arrow."

"I don't think so. The only hold I have over August so far is that wagon train."

"Think on it a mite more, Captain," said Slocum. "Why would any wagonmaster stay unless he was honest?"

"I can't prove August is behind this, but there are rumors about him down in Texas. A few of my men think they remember him. I've sent wires to the authorities asking."

Slocum kept a poker face. If Hawkins went to such lengths for Jethro, he had also sent some wires about him.

"I'd like to talk to Dantley again. I doubt I can make him talk, but maybe he'll tell you Jethro has nothing to do with the robbery."

"Can't say I'd believe a snake in the grass like Dantley, but go on. Just don't disturb me—and a guard's going to be on duty just inside the door. Don't try anything foolish."

"Not me, Captain."

Slocum stood outside the crude jail cell and peered in at Dantley. The man huddled in the corner. They hadn't bothered giving him a blanket, and the straw gave scant protection against the chilly spring nights.

"You again?" Dantley rolled over and tried to ignore Slocum.

"I know who your boss is," Slocum said.

This got a strong reaction from the prisoner. He surged to his feet and gripped the bars. "You're lying."

"No, I'm not. I just watched a daylight robbery of the Tahlequah bank. I know who's hiding behind that red bandanna and duster."

"You come to get me out?"

"I want you to tell Captain Hawkins that Jethro August has nothing to do with any of the robberies. Blame Brighton and Villalobos for everything. They're beyond the cavalry's reach." Slocum didn't want to tell Dantley what had happened to his two friends. He might refuse to say anything at all out of fear.

"I've tried. He won't buy any of it." Dantley pressed closer to the bars and lowered his voice so the guard couldn't hear. "Get me out. Don't let me rot in here."

"Tell Captain Hawkins that Jethro had nothing to do with the robberies and we'll see."

"You don't want me to peach on the boss?" A sly look came to the outlaw's face. "Of course you don't. I understand it all now. You *do* know the boss. Pretty good, unless I miss my guess."

"I got some work to do," Slocum said. "Talk to the captain, and we'll see about getting you free." He paused, remembering Grace's message to the robber. "I almost forgot to tell you. The preacher forgives you for all your sins."

"All?" Dantley's eyes glowed.

"That's mighty big forgiving, if you ask me," Slocum said.

Slocum had done what he could to get the wagon train moving, but he didn't think Hawkins would believe Dantley's confession. If anything, the cavalry officer might think Slocum had something to do with the robberies, too.

Slocum went to the adjutant's office. The lieutenant put in long hours, too, working on a stack of reports.

"Captain Hawkins said you were nosing around again. What can I do for you?" the young officer asked in exasperation.

"Just wanted to check the posters again."

"Got a faulty memory? Or you looking for someone else this time?"

"Can't rightly remember," Slocum said, touching the side of his head where Doc Cliett had put a plaster.

"Go on," the adjutant said in disgust. He pored over his reports while Slocum went through the two-foot stack. He found the smeary poster for William Deutsch and tried to decide how best to get it out of the pile. It was brittle with age and well nigh illegible, but Wingate had recognized the preacher, and Hawkins might, also.

Slocum put the poster to one side where he could get it if the adjutant's attention shifted out of the office for even a few seconds. A complete search failed to show any old posters on him for judge killing. He heaved a sigh of relief on this score. And Jethro August didn't have one detailing the problems he'd had down in Texas. Slocum hadn't expected to find any, since Hawkins would have used this to arrest Jethro immediately.

But how could he get the preacher's fifteen-year-old wanted poster out of the office?

Just as he was about to try some sleight of hand, a disturbance outside brought the adjutant around in his chair. He looked at Slocum, then said, "Outside. Now." He hurried out ahead, giving Slocum ample time to stuff the poster inside his shirt.

The adjutant locked the office door and rushed away, forgetting Slocum. Slocum took the time to strike a lucifer and put it to the poster. The flame consumed the old paper in seconds. He hoped this ended the need to protect Cole Mason from the authorities.

Then he went to see what it was that had caused such a ruckus. He went cold inside when he overheard the Western Union clerk's comment to Captain Hawkins.

"He looked like a drowned rat. I swear, though, I never seen a man that big or what smelled that bad. And he threatened to break my neck if I didn't send the wire for him. He didn't have any money, but I couldn't say no."

"Who did he wire?" asked the cavalry commander.

"St. Louis for information on William Deutsch. He signed the wires Wingate."

Slocum cursed. How had the bounty hunter survived? The metal plates he wore should have dragged him straight to the bottom of the raging river. The man had to be like a cat and have nine lives. Slocum had claimed a couple. How many did he have left?

"What was the answer?" asked Hawkins.

"I didn't understand it. It said something about expiring five years back."

"There's no current warrant out for William Deutsch?"

"Reckon that was the gist of it, Captain. It surely didn't set well with Wingate. He smashed my key and tore up the place something fierce. I was afraid to say a word to him.

He stormed out and disappeared in the direction of the saloon. What you gonna do about this? It's gonna cost at least a hundred dollars to get the office repaired. Until then, there's not going to be any messages going or coming."

"Wingate's at the saloon?" Hawkins turned to the adjutant. "Lieutenant," he ordered, "take a squad—make that *two*—and bring Wingate in. You don't have to be gentle with the son of a bitch."

"We won't take any chances, sir," the officer said. The adjutant hurried off to obey.

"Who's gonna pay for the repair work, Captain? I'm not doing it out of my pocket. I don't have that kind of money."

"How long will it be until another office decides something is wrong when you don't respond?"

"I don't know. A few days."

"What happens then?"

"They might send someone to check."

"Then wait. Fort Gibson can do without a telegraph for a day or two. Now, if you'll let us get about our business, we'll try to stop Wingate from tearing up the entire town."

Slocum slipped out of the fort and stood in deep shadows where he could see the front of the saloon. Even though he had seen Wingate die, it hardly surprised him to find that the Western Union clerk's identification had been accurate. Six soldiers fought to hold Pisser Wingate's arms as they dragged him from the saloon.

They dragged the fighting bounty hunter into the stockade. Slocum leaned against the stockade wall and listened intently when Captain Hawkins confronted Wingate.

"You've made a nuisance of yourself, Mr. Wingate. We're going to let you cool off in lockup."

"I got proof!" bellowed Wingate. "William Deutsch has

been robbing banks left and right. You can't ignore it."

"The telegraph clerk said your reply from St. Louis indicated no current warrant exists for this Deutsch fellow. You are creating a tempest in a teapot, and I will not have it in Fort Gibson."

"He robbed your goddamn bank. He did!"

Slocum groaned. Wingate couldn't have said anything more likely to get the cavalry officer's attention.

"He is not a figment of your imagination?" asked Hawkins.

"He's with the damned wagon train. He's got to be. Why else do they keep me from prowling around and looking for him?"

"I can think of several reasons," Hawkins said, sniffing loudly. Slocum almost laughed at this but didn't when he realized what was happening. Hawkins was still listening to the bounty hunter. That was bad news for Cole Mason.

"He's there. Don't go denying it."

"You have proof?"

"Find Deutsch and you'll find the loot. He's the one behind all the robberies from here to Arkansas."

Slocum wanted to shout out how Wingate had come by that information, to tell Captain Hawkins about Brighton and Villalobos, but he held his peace. He could better serve Mason—and his daughter—by hightailing it back to the wagon train and warning him.

Grace would have to learn of her father's other profession. What galled Slocum the most was how the preacher had lied to him. With a straight face he had said he hadn't robbed any banks since Grace was eight years old.

Slocum found his sorrel and climbed into the saddle. The euphoria he had felt earlier had disappeared. Pisser Wingate was still alive and still a thorn in the side—a deadly thorn, to boot. The best way of dealing with him was to run, and that was what Slocum intended to do. He wasn't afraid of Wingate, but he had learned the value of retreating to fight again another day.

As Slocum rode toward the edge of town, he slowed and eventually reined to a halt. He frowned as he looked back over his shoulder at the fort. Something moving in the shadows near the rear caught his attention. He wheeled around and sat, staring intently into the inky blackness as if this might penetrate the night.

A flash of dim light on blued steel brought him up in his stirrups, alert and curious. The guard pacing a slow circuit on the wall ten feet above the man hiding in the fort's shadow heard nothing. He didn't even pause to investigate.

"Damn," Slocum said when he figured out what was happening. "Mason is one audacious son of a bitch."

Hacking sounds filled the night. No one in the stockade heard them over Pisser Wingate's bellowing as he was put into a cell. For a few minutes, Mason stopped work. Only when Wingate had quieted down did he resume work on the stockade wall.

Slocum found himself torn by indecision. When Dantley got free, Mason would learn everything that had happened in Fort Gibson. That relieved Slocum of any obligation he felt to warn the preacher about Wingate. What he did after he got his cohort free was his own business. If he had any sense, he'd head for the high country. California's Sierra Madres might not be far enough to keep Pisser Wingate from following, but it would be a start.

A wrenching sound filled the night. This caused sentries in the fort to awaken from their slumber. Carbines cocked and angry soldiers shouted.

Slocum heard Dantley whoop in glee as he squeezed through the opening his boss had made in the stockade wall. Then everything was dwarfed by Wingate's angry shouts.

Soldiers appeared on the stockade walls, rifles ready.

Dantley got on the spare horse Mason had brought along. The two outlaws raced off into the night. Slocum saw long tongues of flame leap from the muzzles of the soldiers' rifles. From the way the fleeing men rode, he doubted either had been hit.

All hell broke loose when Captain Hawkins got his company together. Bugles sounded and horses neighed loudly. A clanking of swords preceded Hawkins and his adjutant as they rode from the fort at the heads of two long columns of soldiers. This time they intended to get their bank robbers.

Slocum spat when he saw Pisser Wingate following Captain Hawkins's column on a strong cavalry mount. Either he had escaped or Hawkins had released him when Dantley escaped.

Turning back in the direction of Jethro August's wagon train, Slocum rode out at a brisk pace. He wanted to tell Grace why her father wasn't likely to return. He thought it was better if he told her than if she found it out from Hawkins or Wingate.

He rode only a half mile before the memory of how Pisser Wingate had bushwhacked him returned. He couldn't let this go unpunished. He had thought the bounty hunter dead.

Slocum reversed his course and headed back into Fort Gibson. The trail left by Captain Hawkins's troopers—and Wingate—wouldn't be hard to find. He would settle accounts with the huge back-shooter once and for all.

13

Even though it was darker than a well digger's destination, Slocum had no trouble finding the road taken by the cavalry. Dust hung in the springtime air and pointed like an arrow in the right direction. He had no idea if they were on the trail of the two fugitives, but he didn't care.

He wanted Pisser Wingate dead.

Slocum slowed and dismounted when he came to a fork in the road. Mason and Dantley had ridden to the north when they left Fort Gibson. One small road, more a trail, cut toward the west while the main road continued to the north and east toward Flat Rock Ford. Slocum tried to decide which road Wingate might have taken.

There was no way of telling. The key to finding Wingate was to find Mason. He sat back on his haunches and tried to figure out what Mason had in mind. The preacher was nobody's fool. He had shown daring with the single-handed daylight bank robbery in Tahlequah and Dantley's rescue. Where was he most likely to go?

"Grace," Slocum decided. "His daughter's the key. He'll try to get back to her." From this idea he worked out the best route for the preacher to take. Going northeast to Flat Rock Ford or Union Mission got him nowhere. He'd have to cross the Verdigris River and then the Grand River just to swing around to go south to return to the stalled wagon train.

Slocum looked toward the west along the smaller road. The Arkansas River might pose a problem with its currents swollen by spring runoff, but not that much of one. They had crossed the Arkansas once. Mason might think he knew the river better than the other two.

Slocum mounted and rode west along the narrow road. In less than an hour of steady riding, he overtook Captain Hawkins—and Wingate.

Approaching cautiously, he was able to overhear the men arguing. Wingate stayed low to the ground, a lucifer held aloft to cast light on the trail. Hawkins refused to believe the bounty hunter was capable of finding a track in the darkness.

". . . God's truth, Captain. Get down here and look. Tell me if what I'm seein' ain't the right trail."

Hawkins dismounted and knelt. Slocum sat back and watched as they argued over the meaning of the trail Wingate had found. Eventually, the cavalry officer agreed.

"Men, this way!" He led his troop off the road and toward a steep shale-dotted embankment to the west that Slocum guessed was the Arkansas River.

When they had gone, he trotted to the spot Wingate had examined so carefully for a closer look.

Slocum considered what facts—and suppositions—he had about Cole Mason. The man was clever. Slocum stayed on foot and began circling the area. In ten minutes he found new tracks leading at right angles to the direction taken by Captain Hawkins and his soldiers. Mason had laid a false trail. In the darkness, it had fooled even an experienced tracker like Wingate.

Slocum reckoned that Mason had headed west toward the curving river for a few hundred yards, then dragged a bush behind his horse to hide when he changed direction and turned south. Slocum had found the tracks where Mason abandoned the bush in favor of speed and convenience. When he discovered two sets of horses' tracks fifteen minutes later, he knew he had outfoxed the preacher.

Cole Mason had to ford the Arkansas to get back to the wagon train and his daughter, but he'd be crossing ten miles to the south of Hawkins and his men. If the cavalry officer twigged to the deception and wanted to come directly after the bank robber, he'd have to ford the oxbowing Arkansas twice, slowing him down.

Not for the first time, Slocum felt real admiration for Mason's cleverness. The only problem he had with the man and his thieving ways was being lied to. Slocum couldn't get over his anger at swallowing the yarn hook, line, and sinker; he had really thought the preacher had been telling the truth about not giving up his life of crime.

Knowing that Cole Mason had eluded Hawkins and the troopers presented Slocum with a problem. He had trailed them this far for a chance to kill Wingate. With their prey off in another direction, Wingate wasn't likely to find Mason.

Slocum had lost his bait.

His fingers drummed on the butt of his Colt, then he came to a decision. He would follow Mason and let Wingate wait for another day. He didn't think he had seen the last of the huge bounty hunter.

After a half-hour ride, he approached the river with caution, not sure where the muddy banks began. He didn't want to tumble, sorrel and rider, into the raging river. To his surprise, the river widened considerably and turned shallow to give a good place to ford. Slocum wondered if Mason had been lucky or if he had scouted this area and knew how easily crossed the river was. Planning and daring seemed to be Mason's strong points. Slocum decided the preacher had known where he was running to. Dantley's rescue from the Fort Gibson stockade had been daring, but not as foolhardy as it had first appeared.

Slocum crossed without a problem, then dismounted and walked along the riverbank for a half mile. He found the spot where two horses had emerged from the river. He dropped to his hands and knees and examined the tracks as carefully as he could. Back where Wingate and Hawkins had been fooled, Slocum had noticed that one horse's shoe had a deep notch in it. He tried to find the notch mark but couldn't. The muddy banks swallowed any such clue to the riders' identity.

Following the trail inland a few hundred yards gave Slocum a clear hoofprint. He smiled. He was still following Mason and Dantley.

He continued walking his horse to give the sorrel a much needed rest. He was glad that he had. The two horses parted company, one going straight east and the other continuing south. Slocum tried to figure out which of the tracks belonged to Mason. He didn't care about Dantley. The man could grow wings and fly away for all he cared.

But he had a powerful lot to discuss with the preacher.

Slocum decided to follow the horse with the notched shoe. He had an even chance that this was Mason's, and he had been lucky up to this point.

The terrain turned rougher, and Slocum remained on

foot to keep the tracks in view. Another hour of hard tracking showed a reunion of the two riders. Slocum wondered where Mason had gone. It didn't matter that he had the two of them together again. Dantley was a follower and would do whatever he was told.

Wood smoke caught on a vagrant breeze made his nostrils flare. When a scream cut through the still night, Slocum's hand flashed to his Colt Navy.

He had heard such agony before—and not long ago. When Brighton had been skinned alive, he had made noises just like these. Slocum tethered his horse and drew his pistol before walking softly upwind.

More sounds of abject pain set his teeth on edge. He dared not hurry. To reveal himself without knowing what was happening was a sure way to end up with his own hide hanging from a tree limb. Slocum slipped behind a large-boled oak and peered into a small clearing. It took several seconds for his eyes to adjust to the bright light from the campfire.

His gorge rose when he saw Pisser Wingate standing over Dantley, the thick-bladed bowie knife in his hand. The firelight caught the bloody smears on the knife. The bounty hunter was again working out his vicious nature on another human being.

"Stop lying," Wingate bellowed. "Tell me the truth and you'll be a better man for it."

Dantley moaned something Slocum couldn't hear. Wingate roared in rage and thrust his knife into the campfire until it glowed a dull red. He pressed the side of the blade into Dantley's groin. The man had been tied to the ground spread-eagle. He strained against his bonds but couldn't escape the torture.

"That's as hot as it's ever been there, ain't it, boy? Now quit your lyin' and confess everything. Tell me William

Deutsch is responsible for all the robberies."

"He isn't!" shrieked Dantley. The knife sliced off an ear. Slocum saw the severed flesh arc up, disappear into the night, and then land in the fire to sizzle and pop.

"Maybe you don't know him by that name. Look at this picture. Tell me who it is. Tell me it's the man who planned all your robberies. Tell me, damn you!"

Wingate held up a tattered wanted poster. Even from twenty yards away, Slocum knew the picture was worthless. The bounty hunter had carried it too long in his pocket. The poster in the Fort Gibson adjutant's office had been yellow and brittle with age. This one was almost worn blank.

"Mason?" croaked Dantley.

"Mason? Is that the moniker he uses now? What's his first name? Tell me!" The knife came down again. Dantley screeched like a scalded hound dog.

"Cole Mason," Dantley sobbed.

Slocum had enough. He wasn't going to let Wingate torture another man to death, but a twenty-yard shot in the dark was chancy. He wanted Pisser Wingate dead. How the man had left the cavalry squad, circled around, got ahead of Slocum, and had time to do this to Dantley was beyond understanding. But then, Wingate had escaped certain death in the raging river.

Slocum aimed, then stopped. He had to know if Wingate still wore his body armor. The metal plate had proven too effective in stopping the small-caliber bullets in the past. As quickly as he considered a head shot, he discarded the notion as a flight of fancy. With a good rifle, he could do it, but even with his precision Colt Navy, the shot was too difficult for a six-shooter.

Slocum darted from one tree to another to get as close as possible before showing himself. He wasn't above shoot-

ing Wingate in the back. What the man did to his prisoners
didn't merit giving him a chance to defend himself. He was
an animal.

He finally got into position ten yards to Wingate's right.
This time the bounty hunter wouldn't walk away from the
fight. Slocum had missed his chance before to kill him.
Not now.

Slocum paused for a moment to look at Dantley. The
man lay twitching feebly on the ground. Wingate had
placed him so that the soles of his feet were in the fire. The
flesh had blackened, and the stench made Slocum's lip
curl. Dantley would never walk again on those charred
stumps, even if he didn't die from the other wounds Wingate had inflicted with such savagery.

Another count against Pisser Wingate.

Just as Slocum started to move against the man, he saw
a flicker of movement across the clearing.

Cole Mason stepped into view, wearing his bandanna
pulled up over his nose and his canvas duster flapping
open.

"Deutsch?" called Wingate. "Is that you? Or are you
going by the name Mason now? I don't rightly care what
you call yourself. I'm gonna do to you what I just did to
this pile of shit."

Mason pulled back the duster to show the old black-
powder Remington tucked into his belt.

"That's the way you want it, eh?" Wingate turned so
that Slocum saw his face silhouetted by the campfire. His
jaw tensed, and his hand slid to his side—he was preparing to throw the big bowie knife.

Slocum lifted his Colt and fired just as Mason drew his
Remington. The black-powder pistol discharged and left a
thick cloud of smoke hanging in the air between him and
the bounty hunter.

Slocum didn't know where the preacher's bullet had gone. He had taken careful aim and put his slug through the bounty hunter's skull. From the way Wingate's head snapped to the side, Slocum knew he had fired the killing round.

The gray smoke slowly dissipated. Slocum saw Mason standing on the far side of the clearing, the old Remington still pointed in Wingate's direction. The preacher seemed in shock.

14

Slocum lowered his Colt and started to step out into the firelight. He stopped when he saw Mason approaching, the ancient Remington held out at arm's length. The way his hand shook, Mason might fire at anything that moved. Slocum stayed behind the tree and watched.

Mason went to the fallen bounty hunter, reached down hesitantly to touch his face, and brought away a gloved hand covered with blood. From behind the distinctive red bandanna came the muffled words, "I killed him."

Slocum was puzzled by Mason's shocked reaction. The man had shown audacity at every turn. Somewhere during his bank-robbing career he must have shot a man or two. He carried a sawed-off shotgun during some robberies for more than show. Slocum shrugged off the preacher's peculiar reaction as having to do with his finding religion. It struck Slocum as odd that Mason could rob with impunity but killing took the starch right out of him.

"Help me," moaned Dantley.

Slocum started out into the clearing again but held back. He wanted to see what Mason did for the tortured man.

"I'm sorry," he heard Mason say. Again the words were so low he could barely hear.

"Help me. I hurt. God, I hurt!" pleaded Dantley. The man strained weakly against his bonds. Mason took Wingate's fallen knife and cut the ropes on Dantley's wrists. The man rolled onto his side and began to cry.

Mason stood and stared at the man for several seconds as if coming to an unpleasant decision. Then the old Remington lifted and sighted. Again the gun bucked and thick smoke filled the clearing. By the time it blew away, Mason had vanished.

Slocum hurried out, six-shooter in hand. Of the masked outlaw leader, he saw no trace. Cole Mason had shot his remaining cohort and then fled into the night.

Kneeling, Slocum examined Dantley. Mason's slug had caught him just above the remaining ear, killing him instantly. Slocum nodded in approval. Dantley would have been a hideously deformed cripple if he had lived—and that was a mighty big if. Slocum doubted anyone could have saved him. Mason had given his friend the best gift possible: quick death.

Again his opinion of Mason rose. The man didn't hesitate when it came to doing a difficult task.

Slocum had seen men who would have lugged Dantley miles to try to get him to a doctor rather than admit nothing could be done. Cole Mason had accurately judged the man's injuries.

What irked Slocum was how Mason ran away without giving Dantley a proper burial. Slocum looked around the grassy clearing and found a likely place for a grave. He didn't have anything but a fallen branch to dig with, but the earth was damp and soft enough to scoop out an adequate burial pit. Twenty minutes' hard work and Slocum was ready to put Dantley to rest.

With some distaste, he dragged the man over and rolled him into the grave.

"It wasn't worth it," Slocum said over the body. "It never is." With those brief words, he scooped the dirt up and dropped it on the uncaring body. He wiped the sweat from his forehead when he had finished mounding the earth over Dantley. Then he stood and looked back toward the guttering, low campfire.

"You get to rot in the sun when it comes up," he said to Wingate. "I doubt if even the buzzards want your stinking carcass."

Slocum froze when the last word left his lips. He drew his six-shooter and stalked back to the dying campfire.

"Son of a bitch!" he cried. "He's gone! Why can't I kill that bastard?"

He crouched and worked quickly, making sure all six cylinders carried a load. Slocum didn't believe in the supernatural, but Pisser Wingate's longevity was beginning to spook him a mite. The man couldn't drown. He had been shot down twice. Slocum had explained one time by the metal armor Wingate had worn—but that wasn't true this time. Slocum had aimed for the head and had hit him.

"Why didn't he die?"

Slocum dropped to his hands and knees to begin his systematic search. He wasn't going to leave until he'd finished Wingate off once and for all.

The puddle of blood from the bounty hunter's wound had turned the soft loam to a sticky mud that clung to his fingers when he touched it. When Slocum found a trail of dark blood leading off into the woods, he knew that his aim had been off a hair. The bullet hadn't done any better job than Wingate's had done on him.

Broken limbs and crushed undergrowth showed Slocum the trail as surely as if Wingate had splashed whitewash to mark his path. He advanced slowly, not sure that the bounty hunter wasn't laying a deadly trap for him. Slocum had come to expect anything from the man. Anything.

Remembering how Wingate had attacked before, Slocum spent a good portion of his time looking up into the overhanging tree limbs. He didn't know how the man could have the strength to get up there, but he took no chances.

Wingate had been drowned and shot repeatedly and was still alive. It amazed Slocum how pure meanness could keep a man going, but it did for the bounty hunter.

The first light of false dawn turned the sky purple and gray. Using it aided Slocum in his search for Wingate. Like a wounded bull, Wingate had charged through the thicket. Nothing slowed him.

Slocum found him by the river, bathing his head wound.

Under other circumstances, Slocum might have given his victim the courtesy of a goodbye before shooting. This time he simply drew his pistol and fired.

Wingate bellowed in rage and fear, turning to face his surprise attacker. Slocum stared into pure animal hatred. Wingate's eyes were huge and bloodshot, rimmed in white like the eyes of a frightened horse. He reared up like a grizzly bear and sent droplets of blood spinning through the air.

Slocum saw that he had hit the bounty hunter a glancing blow with his bullet back in the clearing. A long, shallow, bloody crease ran across the man's forehead. The impact must had thrown him to the ground, knocking him out.

But a clean kill still eluded Slocum. Wingate charged

forward. Slocum stood his ground, firing deliberately. Three shots hit the man in the chest. Slocum didn't hear any *ping* of lead against metal armor plating. The bullets found fleshy berths in Wingate's chest.

And still the man came on. His prodigious strength and fanatical determination gave him a vitality Slocum had never seen in a human being before.

"I'll kill you, boy. You aren't doing me in. Not me! Not Pisser Wingate!"

Slocum's Colt came up empty, the hammer landing on a spent chamber. Then he had his hands full of thrashing, fighting, clawing, biting bounty hunter.

Wingate bowled him over. Slocum rode the wave of smelly buckskin and rolled with it, getting Wingate thrown over to one side. Slocum found it hard to hang on to the man because of the blood pouring down the front of his skin shirt.

"You're in cahoots with Mason, aren't you, boy? I'll kill the lot of you. You conspired with the lawmen and the damned corrupt judges to get your names taken off the posters. You won't escape justice. You won't escape *me!*"

Slocum didn't waste breath arguing. He picked up a rock and smashed it into the side of Wingate's head with all his strength. The blow failed to land squarely. A long tear of bloody flesh peeled from Wingate's pate. Nothing slowed the man or robbed him of his superhuman strength.

"Mason!" roared the bounty hunter. "I'll track down the murderin' son of a bitch." He backhanded Slocum, knocking him to the ground. Slocum slipped on the muddy riverbank trying to stand. He rolled and found himself sliding down a steep slope toward the churning river. When he hit the water, he sucked in a lungful of air in time to keep from drowning.

The cold water snapped him to full consciousness. He

fought the strong current and grabbed a log jutting out from
the bank. A few seconds to gather his strength was all it
took. He kicked hard and pulled himself up and onto the
bank. Before he returned to where he had left Wingate, he
picked up a long limb that had floated down the river and
hefted it.

It made a good enough club to bash in the giant's head.

"Where are you, you stinking owlhoot?" Slocum cried.
Pisser Wingate was nowhere to be seen.

Slocum sank to the ground and picked up his empty
pistol. Wingate had gotten away from him once more.

But Slocum knew where the bounty hunter had gone.
Wounded as he was, he had only one thought—to kill
William Deutsch.

He had to return to the wagon train and warn Cole
Mason. With a resolute moan, Slocum got to his feet and
retraced his steps through the copse until he found his pa-
tiently waiting sorrel.

He climbed into the saddle aching and still soggy from
his plunge into the river. Slocum stretched and then headed
back toward the wagon train. The dawn broke on a new
Oklahoma day that would have been perfect if it hadn't
been for Pisser Wingate. All the way to the encampment,
Slocum cursed his foul luck. How the bounty hunter had
evaded death so many times was a mystery.

It couldn't happen too many more times or Cole Mason
would find himself tortured and dead beside the road.
Wingate had found that the old warrants for William
Deutsch were no good, and this seemed to have driven the
man crazy as a doodlebug and made him even more dangerous than he had been.

The sight of the smoke from the early morning cooking
fires didn't cheer Slocum. Wingate might have beat him
back here. Although the bounty hunter couldn't know for

certain where the wagon train was, it didn't require much skill to ask a few of the farmers along the way and get an answer. Wingate wasn't likely to take mute silence as an answer from anyone.

Slocum rode around the perimeter of the camp looking for traces of Mason's horse. He found what might be the tracks coming from due west. Instead of reporting what had happened to Jethro, he rode directly to Mason's wagon.

A lathered horse stood behind the wagon. Of the preacher Slocum saw no trace. He dismounted and went to examine the hot, tired horse more carefully.

"Is there something I can do for you, Mr. Slocum?" came the preacher's ringing tones from inside the wagon. He was sprawled out in a union suit on the soft mattress where Slocum had made love to Grace Mason. Beside the mattress lay an opened Bible.

"You ought to know something, preacher," Slocum said. "Wingate isn't dead. You thought you shot him with your Remington. You missed."

"Sir, I don't know—"

"I was standing in the shadows to his side. I fired at him. I only grazed him. I swear the man has more lives than a cat. You hightailed it, and I went hunting for him after burying Dantley."

Slocum scowled at the preacher's expression. The man was a great actor. Shock and outrage showed on his face in what would have been a believable act if Slocum hadn't seen everything with his own eyes.

"Dantley is dead?"

"You know damned good and well Wingate skinned him and tortured him, just as he did Brighton. Villalobos is the only one of your henchmen to get off easy. Wingate is in such a mood that I don't even want to think what he'll do when he catches you."

"Why should he come after me now?" Mason sat up and began pulling on his black pants, then the stiff shirt with the wide collar he wore when he preached.

"Dantley identified the poster picture of William Deutsch as being you."

"Dantley is in the Fort Gibson lockup. You told me yourself."

"Give it up, Mason," Slocum said angrily. "I watched you bust him out of Captain Hawkins' cell. Wingate is coming after you, and you don't have many choices."

"He thinks I committed the new robberies," Mason said, almost to himself. "The old warrant won't hold, so he's trying to frame me for the more recent crimes."

"Frame you, like hell," said Slocum, totally pissed now. "I *saw* you rob the Tahlequah bank. A nice piece of work it was, and I led the sheriff and his posse away from your trail to pay you back for not gunning me down when you had the chance. All bets are off now. If you want to keep on living, either figure a way to drygulch Wingate or get moving."

"I've done nothing."

Slocum looked at the preacher with nothing but contempt. He vaulted into the wagon and pushed through the meager belongings until he found the case for the black-powder Remington. He opened it and sniffed at the muzzle.

It had been fired recently.

"Here's evidence. The tuckered-out horse is evidence. Do I have to keep looking until I find the red bandanna, the duster, and a pile of loot from the banks?" Slocum tossed the Remington down in disgust. He had no more time for the preacher.

"Mr. Slocum, one question."

"What?"

"Why are you doing this for me?"

"I'm not. I'm doing it for Grace—and for myself. Wingate bushwhacked me. I don't cotton to that, no matter who does it."

"I see," Mason mused. "For Grace."

Slocum snorted and jumped out of the wagon bed. He looked around for the woman but didn't find her. She might be off doing chores while her father pretended to have been asleep all night long. She might not even have noticed that he was gone if she had slept outside by the campfire. Slocum saw a slight indentation in the dirt to show that she might have done that very thing.

He heaved a sigh, hitched up his gunbelt, and went to find Jethro August. He had too much to tell the wagon-master and too little time to do it. Slocum wasn't going to bet on how long it would take Pisser Wingate to find the wagon train. He wanted to be long gone when that hour arrived.

15

Slocum found Jethro August at his small campfire opening a can of beans. To one side he had an unopened can of peaches. He looked up when he heard Slocum. "John! I was beginning to worry. You've been gone so damned long, I thought you'd taken my money and headed for parts unknown. Would have thought that if'n I didn't know you better."

"You haven't paid me yet," Slocum pointed out. He settled down beside the tiny fire and tired to warm his hands from its chary heat. He wasn't successful.

"The damned bonus money will be my death yet," Jethro said with a trace of bitterness. "I need to get the bonus for finding these good people homesteads. How did Hawkins react when you begged him to let me come on through?"

"I didn't beg," Slocum said. "There's good news and some bad. I spoke with Dantley. He was going to tell the captain you had nothing to do with the robberies."

"That's what was holding us up?" Jethro shook his head. Then a worried expression passed like a cloud over him. "They diggin' a lot down Texas way? Most of what happened there won't stand up under official scrutiny."

"Some of Hawkins's troopers seem to remember a dust-up involving you. The reports aren't back yet and may not ever show up." Slocum went on to tell about how Pisser Wingate had bullied the telegraph clerk and wrecked the Western Union office.

"They might not be able to get telegrams in or out for a week or more. Is that good?" Jethro asked.

"Probably. But what's not too good is that Dantley escaped—and he's dead." Slocum finished the story while Jethro ate slowly from the can of beans. He didn't seem to notice that he hadn't finished heating them. When he had licked up the last bit of sauce, he reached for the peaches and used his knife on the lid. Sticky syrup slopped out. Jethro sucked at it. He buried his knife in the ground in way of cleaning its blade.

"What're the odds we can just pull up and go on into Broken Arrow?" he asked after downing two slices of peaches. "The cavalry has its hands full huntin' down their escaped bank robbers. Think they'd even notice one fat ole Texas wagonmaster had moved on through and didn't bother asking?"

"That's up to you to decide," Slocum said. "I got worries of my own. Wingate is still alive and meaner than a polecat with his tail being chewed on."

"You aren't abandonin' me, are you, John?"

"You know me. I don't run, but I'm no fool, either. It's not as if I haven't tried dealing with the bounty hunter." Slocum remembered dragging him from the wagon train and hanging him by his heels. That ought to have been enough warning for any man. Not for Wingate. Slocum still marveled at how the sorrel had kicked him in the head, the many times he had been shot, the drowning in the Arkansas River—all of it—and how the bounty hunter had remained alive and ornery.

"Reckon I can't blame you a whole lot," Jethro allowed. "Wish you would stick it out with us, though. I can use your help gettin' these sodbusters over to the Broken Arrow land office."

"I know, the faster they get their land, the sooner you get your delivery bonus."

"You'd have more guns at your back stayin' than goin'," Jethro pointed out. "Wingate is one mean son of a bitch, but he's only human. Enough lead in him will stop him dead in his tracks. Even if he wore that fancy-ass metal plate you told me about, he'd be dead if we pounded at him hard enough."

Slocum had heard of Navajos infected with ghost sickness—*tchindi*, they called it. The afflicted people turned into animals and raced under the moon and were impossible to kill except by magic. He didn't believe much of this, but after seeing Wingate's vitality, a bit of doubt had crept into his head on the matter. The bounty hunter might be a *tchindi* grizzly bear.

"You're almost there, and I've done what I can. I'm leaving, Jethro."

"Hate to see it, but I understand. You're too good a friend to lose, John." Jethro finished off the last slice of peach and tossed the can into the fire. "I'd surely like to pay you, you know I would. But the money's just not ridin' high in my pocket right now. What advance money the sodbusters paid all went for supplies, pay for those worthless bank-robbin' sons of bitches, for other things. Had to bribe a few lawmen along the way, too, to get right-of-way for passage. A damned nuisance, and expensive, John. You know that."

"That's all right. I'll catch up with you later and collect what's owed me."

"Let me know where you'll be in a month. I'll have the money then and can wire you what's due."

Slocum shook his head. He wanted to simply vanish from sight. He doubted Wingate would hang around and spy on Jethro August, but wiring money might be dangerous. The bounty hunter had gotten one Western Union clerk to talk. He could get another to spill everything he knew with little trouble.

Pisser Wingate was intimidating.

Slocum found himself facing another dilemma. He didn't know if he should tell the entire story to his friend. Jethro deserved to know how Cole Mason had used the wagon train—and Dantley, Brighton, and Villalobos—as cover for his robbing ways. In a way, the preacher had acted as a magnet for most of the bad luck plaguing Jethro August on the journey.

If it hadn't been for the string of bank robberies, the trio of scouts wouldn't have been arrested. And if William Deutsch hadn't been involved so disastrously with Wingate more than a decade earlier, the bounty hunter would never have come swooping down on them like some giant bird of prey.

Still, he had warned Mason about Wingate. If the preacher wanted to run, fine. Slocum could do no more. With only a few days left between the Broken Arrow homestead sites and the sodbusters, Jethro had little to worry about from Mason.

Slocum came to his decision. He would say nothing about the preacher's bank robberies, in Tahlequah, Fort Gibson, or anywhere else along the wagon train's route. It didn't concern Jethro and would only cause delay all around. Jethro might even take it into his head to turn the preacher over to Captain Hawkins in way of a bribe for quick passage to Broken Arrow.

"Our paths will cross again," Slocum said.

"Watch your back, John."

"You, too," said Slocum. The men shook hands. Slocum hurried off, having done what he'd set out to do. He had given Jethro what information he could, and he had warned the preacher. What the two did now was entirely up to them. He had down as much as he possibly could for each of them. More. Slocum didn't much like risking his neck for no return.

He tended his horse, making sure the sorrel got some grain from the supply wagon. Slocum wanted to curry the faithful animal but decided that time was working against him. He could see to the horse's needs when he got a few miles between him and the wagon train.

He rubbed the sorrel down, then heaved the saddle into place. The horse protested the weight. She had hoped for a long rest after the night's hard ride.

"Soon we can rest," he told her, patting her strong neck. He made sure she had a lump of sugar as a reward for her patience, then started to mount. A voice calling his name made him hesitate.

"John, where are you going? Papa said you'd just been at our wagon. I'm sorry I missed you then."

Grace Mason stared at him in disbelief as she realized he was leaving.

"You can't go!" she protested.

"I don't know what your pa told you, but you'd better ask him to explain it all to you. You deserve the truth."

"He's not running you off?" she said, wide-eyed and outraged. "He found out about us and is running you off!"

"That's not it." Slocum didn't want to admit that it was the bounty hunter who was making him so skittish. He didn't cotton to the notion of being afraid of any man—but he was beginning to think Pisser Wingate was something more than an ordinary man.

"The bounty hunter?" she asked, her expression still one of incredulity. "I don't believe it. *You?*"

"Me," he said.

"But Wingate's dead," she said.

Slocum started to speak, but Cole Mason's booming voice drowned him out.

". . . perdition is upon us!" he cried. "We must repent now before it is too late. We must prepare for the coming judgment upon us!"

"He's starting in on *that* sermon again," Grace said in exasperation. "John, don't go. Please. Let's go somewhere and talk about this—about us."

She made a persuasive argument. He looked into her blue eyes and felt his resolve to leave melting like snow in the spring. As disgusted with himself for agreeing as he was at Grace for asking him, he pointed toward the stand of trees at the top of the nearby rise. She shook her head.

"We've been up there. Let's go down by the river."

He followed her as she made her way through the camp and down a path worn to dirt over the past few days by the sodbusters as they made their way to the river for water.

"I found a quiet spot where no one will disturb us." She took his hand and led him past large rocks and around the bend in the river. A small, rocky alcove made him think they had become the only people in the world. Mason's sermon was drowned out by the sound of the rushing river. They couldn't see the wagons, and, as Grace had promised, no one was likely to stumble across them. The camp's main watering area lay a hundred yards to the south.

"I was here bathing when you came to camp and spoke with Papa," she said. She dropped down to the slippery rock and took off one shoe. She dipped her dainty foot in the water. "It's just as cold now as it was earlier." Her other shoe followed. Then she began stripping off the rest of her clothing. She seemed oblivious to Slocum and the way he stared.

For several seconds, she stood on the rock and eyed the water. She rubbed her arms in anticipation of what was to come. She flashed him a bright, wicked smile and pulled back her long, dark hair.

Buck naked, she dived into the shallow pool. Silvery beads of water rose in the air around her, turning her into a Greek goddess rising from the depths. She swam powerfully underwater, corkscrewed, and came to her feet, wiping water from her eyes.

Through the crystal-clear water Slocum saw bobbing breasts capped with bright pink nipples and the dark triangle of fleece between the woman's slender legs. Grace turned and floated on her back, then twisted agilely and swam off to the far side of the pool. Just yards away the river ran deep and dangerous. Here they seemed isolated from a world of woe.

"Aren't you going to join me?" she teased. "You look . . . dusty." Grace paddled back toward the center of the pool. "And you must find me attractive or you wouldn't be staring so."

She splashed water at him. Slocum cursed himself for being such a fool. Wingate would descend on the wagon train like a tornado. The safest place when that happened was to be far, far away. Yet he couldn't deny the feelings building inside for Grace.

He stripped off his clothing and poised for a moment on the rock. Grace eyed him with true appreciation. Then he

dived into the pool. The cold water took away his breath
—and then it didn't matter.

Warm arms circled his body and drew him close. He felt
the woman's lush body pressing into his. He responded.
Lips crushing hers, Slocum kissed her until they both
gasped.

"I need you, John. I need you more than I ever have a
man."

She struggled in his arms. Her water-slick body allowed
her to slip away. She dived under the water and surfaced a
few feet away, face flushed with her breasts bobbing de-
lightfully.

"Catch me," she challenged.

"So it's going to be like that again?"

"Afraid you can't do it? Is the cold water robbing you of
your strength?"

Slocum dived under the water and swam powerfully toward her. She tried to get away but couldn't move fast
enough to elude him. His strong hand circled her ankle and
tugged. She slid underneath the surface, sputtering and
thrashing.

His hands worked up her leg, stroking and squeezing.
He parted her thighs to reveal the area most alluring to
him. With a strong kick, he surged up out of the water and
came down. Instinctively, Grace's legs circled his waist.

"You caught me too easily," she protested. But there
was no hint of disappointment in her voice.

A twitch of his pelvis and both of them gasped with
pleasure.

"I . . . can't keep doing it this way," she panted. Every
movement he made sent her face under the gentle waves
rocking from one side of the pool to the other.

Slocum's arms caught her around the waist and heaved
her up and out of the water. He got his feet under him and

widened his stance enough to support both their weights. He lowered her again. Once more they both gasped with the joy of his hot length sinking deeply within her.

Grace threw her arms around his neck and kissed him. Slocum rocked back and forth, the water buoying them. He used the rocking motion to the best advantage.

"Oh, John, this is even better than I thought. It . . . it's incredible!"

He kissed the sweet, deep valley between her firm breasts, licking away at the gooseflesh caused by the icy water. His tongue stroked up one snowy cone of firm flesh and found the coppery button on its crest hard and inviting. He sucked. Grace gasped and clung to him, her legs pulling their bodies even tighter.

"Don't stop," she urged. "I need you so inside me. Please, oh yes, yes!"

He took the hard nipple between his teeth and gently gnawed. His tongue stroked across and teased it. Then he gave the other breast the identical treatment.

Her legs tensed and relaxed, pulling them together and letting the water push them apart in a rhythm that Slocum found exhilarating. The water cupped his balls and provided stimulation he had seldom found before.

Grace stroked through his thick dark hair, then laced her fingers tightly and pulled hard. He groaned as her hips ground down onto his thick, fleshy spike. He couldn't move too much or he would lose his footing on the slippery underwater rocks.

The pressures mounted within his loins. Grace rocked and twisted and moved faster, friction warming them both to the point of no return. Slocum pulled her in and tried to split her apart with his upward thrusting. He lost his balance and sent them both tumbling into the water.

Neither released the other. Like a pair of otters, they

continued their enthusiastic movements until both sputtered and gasped for air. Slocum had spilled his seed, and Grace had shivered through her own intense passion.

Grace kicked twice and floated beside where Slocum drifted on his back. She reached between his legs and massaged the slowly deflating organ.

"That was fabulous, John. I've never felt anything like it."

"The fear of death can give that feeling," he said.

"We weren't about to drown. The bottom's not that far away." Grace stood to prove her point and vanished. She had stepped into a deep hole on the pool's bottom. Slocum dived for her and found that she wasn't hurt, only irritated.

They splashed together to the surface. By the time she got the water out of her eyes and ears, she was laughing.

"This is the most fun I've had in years," she said. Her voice softened. "Maybe these are the best times I've ever had." Her bright blue eyes stared boldly at him.

He kissed her again, as if for the first time. Then they made love in the pool once more.

16

When they had finished, Grace and Slocum swam to the far bank and pulled themselves up onto a large rock. The warm spring sun beat down on their naked bodies and dried them rapidly. Slocum stretched like a lizard and wished this moment could be locked up forever like a bug in amber.

It never happened that way. Whenever he found something worthwhile, it vanished. He sometimes thought he went through life trying to grab a handful of smoke.

Grace reached over and stroked across his chest. She rolled up onto an elbow, ignoring the rock's rough surface, and stared at him. He felt the heat in those brilliant blue eyes.

"I've got to go," he said. "I don't want to, especially now, but I have to."

"Why, John?"

"Pisser Wingate is more than I can handle. I never thought I'd say that about any man, but I'm doing it now.

He's been well nigh impossible to chase off or kill."

"But he's dead!" she exclaimed, a shadow of uneasiness crossing over her beautiful face. "He can't harm you anymore."

She'd said this once before. Slocum stared at her, trying to put together everything he had told her.

"What makes you think Wingate is dead?"

"Why he . . . I . . . you said so."

"No, I didn't."

"John, really—trust me. This Wingate is not going to bother you again."

"How can you be so sure?" Slocum pressed the point. Something about Grace's insistence bothered him. Had her father talked about gunning the bounty hunter down in the clearing after Wingate had killed Dantley? That made no sense. The preacher made such a point of his daughter not knowing about his former bank robberies that he wouldn't confess the latest bout of them with her.

He started to ask again how she was so sure that Wingate was dead when Grace spoke, cutting him off. "I'm worried, John. My father's not been acting normal."

"What do you mean by 'normal'?"

"His sermons are starting to take on the gloom and doom topics like they did after Mama died. He started drinking heavily then, though he's long since stopped on my account."

"How did your ma die?"

Grace shook her head and ran long fingers through her raven-dark, wet hair. "I don't rightly remember. I had a fever. She might have died from the same thing I had. Papa never talks about her death." Grace let out a long sigh. "He never talks about much of anything except preaching. It gets dull."

"You're certainly not what I expected from a preacher's daughter," Slocum said.

"I'm not? How am I different?" She stretched on the rock, lazy and catlike. But no cat had ever looked so attractive.

"Quit fishing for compliments," he said. Slocum's mind drifted, in spite of the woman's naked beauty. He couldn't get Wingate out of his thoughts.

"I'm not dull, am I?" She moved closer, rubbing against him. "I realized a long time ago that I had to find my own excitement. Listening to papa's sermons is so boring, especially when you've heard them a dozen times." She shivered and sat up. "That's what scares me about the way he's preaching now."

"The gloom?"

"He starts preaching brotherhood and forgiveness, switches over to an eye for an eye and ends up with apocalyptic threats of the end of the world."

"Ever since Wingate started nosing around," mused Slocum. He knew what was troubling Cole Mason. He stood up and shook himself dry. The warm Oklahoma sun finished the job quickly. "I'm going."

He stopped and stared at the woman. Her blue eyes were rimmed with tears. Slocum wondered if she would beg him to stay. If she did, it would make things easier. He could walk away knowing she wanted him to stay only for the sake of her father.

Grace Mason said nothing.

Slocum dressed quickly. She came and dressed more slowly. She finally broke the silence. "I'm sorry you have to leave, John. I'm going to miss you terribly."

"You're not going to ask me to stay?"

"No. You've got your reasons. I learned a long time ago to accept what I can't change."

"Hell," he grumbled. "I'll see you and the preacher through to Broken Arrow—or wherever you're going."

"Broken Arrow," she said. "Papa said there wasn't a church there. This will be his first real ministry in almost two years. We've been drifting all that time."

"Just to Broken Arrow," Slocum declared. "Then I've got to get on my way."

"Where?" she asked.

Slocum had no answer for that. Wherever Pisser Wingate wasn't was where he wanted to be.

"Don't know what made you change your mind, John, but I'm durn happy you did," said Jethro August. "You helped out more'n I can say these past three days."

They had forded the Arkansas River with some difficulty, in spite of the shallow ford Slocum had scouted. The spring runoffs had increased in just a few days to the point of making the crossing dangerous. With Slocum's help and expertise they hadn't lost any wagons. Two teams of oxen had drowned, and one horse had broken a leg and had to be destroyed. Of the settlers, all had made it safely.

Slocum had spent the entire time looking over his shoulder. He had no idea what had happened to Pisser Wingate. The bounty hunter wasn't the kind to give up, especially when he scented blood.

Jethro vented a deep sigh and stared at the gently rolling hills around Broken Arrow. "We got here. I've already put in land claims for a half dozen of them sodbusters and collected my bonus money. If you want to be off, I can pay you what's due."

From the wistful way Jethro spoke, Slocum knew his pay would be well nigh all the wagonmaster had collected so far. He had stayed with the wagon train three days longer than he'd anticipated—or was prudent. "I appreciate it, Jethro." Slocum waited for his friend to count out the coins. Jethro started to ask if Slocum would take greenbacks, then bit it off. He knew he wouldn't.

"What are your plans?" Jethro asked when he had parted with the last of the gold.

"I want to ride around and look the place over," Slocum said. "Never been to this part of Oklahoma before."

"Don't see much reason to look it over now," Jethro said. He spat. "The land's all right for growing things. Can't see much else of worth around here. Even the farming's got problems in places. Oil leaks up out of the ground and destroys entire fields. A damned nuisance, if you ask me, but these folks don't seem to mind."

"There's no accounting for a settler's tastes," Slocum agreed. "I might see you again before I hit the trail. If not . . ." Slocum shook hands with Jethro August.

The wagonmaster smiled crookedly and waved him off. Slocum rode slowly into the town, looking over the small collection of buildings and businesses. Broken Arrow had only one saloon and two general stores. That told him much about the countryside. More settlers and their families than ranchers with hands hankering to wet their whistles and let off steam at the end of a tiring month of working the range.

What he didn't see was a church. Cole Mason would fit right in—if he decided to stay. The past three days had been hectic ones. Slocum had barely had a chance to talk with the preacher. Of Grace he had seen plenty and always during the night. The idea of leaving her behind when he rode off began to rankle. Yet what kind of life would she have with him on the trail? She was a preacher's daughter. He was hardly more than a drifter looking for . . . what?

Slocum didn't know. He wasn't even sure he'd know if he found it.

He shook himself to clear his head. He had no right even thinking such things. He circled Broken Arrow, went past their small bank, and rode back to the wagon train. He found Cole Mason working to repack some of the boxes inside his wagon. Slocum dismounted. He had to talk with the man.

"Mr. Slocum," greeted the preacher. "What brings you by?"

"Wanted to ask a question or two," he said. Slocum settled on a box, took out his fixings, and rolled himself a smoke. The time it took getting the cigarette lighted gave him the chance to put his thoughts in order. "Where are you settling down?" he asked.

"What? Why, here in Broken Arrow. Haven't you noticed? They don't have a church."

"I was thinking about Wingate. The man's not going to give up."

"I cannot run from shadows all my life," said Mason. "The wicked flee when no man pursueth. God is on my side. I have been virtuous and tried to lead a good life. If Wingate is able to take this away, then it is ordained by a higher authority."

"He's a vicious killer. I think he's as crazy as a stewed hoot owl. The only way of dealing with him is to shoot him—and even then, there're problems." Slocum shook his head as he remembered how often he had tried to finish off Wingate and had failed.

"Broken Arrow is a nice town. I'm staying."

Slocum started to argue with the preacher and stopped. He puffed at his smoke, then ground it out in the dirt. Mason could be as stupid as he wanted. He knew the facts —and he knew that Captain Hawkins over at Fort Gibson wasn't likely to give up looking for the leader of the bank robbers who had committed the daylight heist and whisked away his prisoner from under his nose.

"Your decision," Slocum said. "But what about Grace? Isn't it going to be dangerous for her when Wingate comes around?"

"She has nothing to fear," Mason snapped. The preacher came over and stared at Slocum with a truculence that startled him. Slocum frowned. The top of Mason's head came to his chin. The man was smaller than most. How did he hope to fight off a man the size of Pisser Wingate?

"I'll be going. I'd advise you to rest on your laurels. Don't try sticking up any more banks."

"Sir, I have not done such in twelve years."

Slocum snorted in disgust. Mason was lying. It made no difference to Slocum. He was leaving all this behind.

But he couldn't leave without first saying goodbye to Grace.

"Where's your daughter?"

"I have to go, Mr. Slocum." Mason spun and stalked off, the Bible firmly tucked under his arm. Slocum watched him go to a stump and climb up on it. He waited a few minutes, then began preaching a hellfire and brimstone sermon.

Slocum started to mount his sorrel and leave. He stopped when a crazy idea came to him. Hearing Cole Mason preach convinced him of the man's sincerity. What if Mason hadn't been lying to him about Dantley and the others?

Slocum looked around. No one noticed him. Those that cared focused their full attention on Mason and his fiery sermon. Slocum slipped into the preacher's wagon and rooted around looking for the presentation case holding the black-powder Remington. It took several minutes of digging, but he found it hidden at the back of a large chest.

Slocum pulled it out. Even before he opened it he knew what he'd find. The case was empty. He closed the case and returned it to its hiding place. He finished his search, hunting everywhere for the red bandanna with the distinctive pattern and the canvas duster he knew that had to be here.

They were all gone.

Slocum slipped from the wagon and mounted his horse. He turned toward the small corral holding the wagon train's animals. He checked through the horses and saw one of Mason's was missing. He slumped forward, head bowed. He tried to think.

"What about the bank?" he muttered aloud. "How would I rob it?" Slocum considered the approaches, where the roads were, the lack of a local sheriff, and the chances for escape.

Escape was low on the list, he decided. Getting into the bank without being seen was more important. The robber already had a hiding place picked out.

Slocum rode slowly toward the eastern edge of town. The road coming in from this direction would give the best approach. As he rode, every sense strained. He was rewarded by the distant sound of a horse neighing and pawing at the ground.

Slocum got his bearings and got off the main road. He went a few yards into a small stand of elm trees, then dismounted. The rest of the way he had to go on foot or he'd spook his prey. Quieter than a hunting cat, he advanced.

Through a tangle of hanging vines he saw Grace Mason. She was dressed only in a thin white cotton chemise. She hummed to herself as she worked on a tiny pack. Slocum didn't have to move much to see her pull out a pair of men's breeches. She rolled the chemise up around her waist and wiggled into the pants. The added fabric around her waist added twenty pounds to her appearance. She put on a man's shirt, then completed the costume by donning the canvas duster and pulling up the red bandanna knotted around her neck.

She took out the black-powder Remington and expertly loaded it. She thrust it into her belt. Then she took out of the pack a sawed-off shotgun Slocum remembered all too well. He had stared down the muzzle of this frightening weapon in the woods after Brighton and Villalobos had been killed.

Cole Mason hadn't spared his life; Grace Mason had.

Slocum marveled at how much she looked like her father when she dressed in men's clothing. For a woman she was tall; her father was short. They were almost the same height. Mounted, Slocum could hardly tell the difference between them, even knowing who rode behind the bandanna and heavy canvas duster.

He tried to blame himself for not before seeing who really rode behind this mask. But he couldn't. Grace had done too good an impersonation.

He had to smile in appreciation. Who would look for a preacher's daughter to rob banks? With Dantley and the other two, she had a decent gang to pull the heists. And her identity explained why Dantley had been so hesitant about naming his boss. Slocum guessed the outlaw had been in love with Grace.

He snorted in disgust. He couldn't fault the man any for that. He hadn't shown any better judgment when it came to Grace. All the facts had been in front of him for some time, but his feelings for her had blinded him to the truth.

She was one hell of a bank robber.

Grace settled into the saddle, checked the way she had

the shotgun slung, touched the butt of the Remington thrust into her belt, then put her heels to the horse. It reared and raced off before Slocum could call out to the woman.

He wanted to warn her against robbing the Broken Arrow bank. It never paid to rob too close to your home. No matter how careful you were, someone would notice sooner or later. Even worse, she was trying this robbery alone, as she had done in Tahlequah. Although it was daring—and for her, exciting—it was as dangerous as anything she could do. Too much could go wrong when pulling a job single-handed.

Slocum sighed and went back to where he'd hitched his sorrel. The horse stared at him quizzically.

"We're not going to *rob* the bank, old girl," he said, patting the horse's neck. "We're just going to make sure nothing happens."

The horse neighed in protest.

"We did this before. Remember how we led the posse astray in Tahlequah? That fat-bellied sheriff had no idea what way the robber went. We did that to keep Grace from learning her father was a bank robber. Seems now we have to do the same thing to keep her father from learning his daughter's one."

The horse didn't understand, and Slocum wasn't even sure *he* did, but he felt a familiar excitement building inside. He had robbed banks in his day and had always gotten a thrill out of it. Sometimes it was from fear, other times from the knowledge that he might get caught. He didn't know why his pulse quickened, and he felt an almost sexual stimulation. Grace must feel the same.

She had bemoaned her dull life. Slocum knew her life hadn't been *that* uninteresting.

Slocum rode steadily toward town. He got to the edge of Broken Arrow just as all hell broke loose. A shotgun blared and glass broke. He picked up the pace and saw Grace running from the bank. She held a small sack in her left hand. The shotgun bucked in her right as she fired off the second barrel to keep those in the bank down and worried.

Grace jumped onto her horse and galloped off in the direction Slocum would have chosen for escape. In this sleepy little town, no one could follow her trail. She was too clever and slippery for that.

Or so he thought until he saw a huge dark form against the general store's wall across the street from the bank. Only one man cast such a large shadow.

Pisser Wingate moved into the sunlight, a determined look on his face. He climbed onto a protesting horse and rode after Grace.

Slocum knew he had no choice. Wingate was a clever and dogged tracker. He thought he was hunting down the man who had been responsible for his brother's death. He would kill without hesitation—and he would kill Grace.

Slocum put his heels into the sorrel's flanks and chased after the other two. Perhaps this time he could finish off the indestructible bounty hunter.

17

John Slocum felt as if his own life depended on catching and stopping Wingate. The bounty hunter whipped his runty horse until its legs threatened to break—and Slocum couldn't narrow the distance between them.

Slocum tried to guess where Grace would slow and change back into her more feminine clothing and once more hide her father's old Remington and shotgun—and the loot. He didn't know the Broken Arrow terrain well enough to ride ahead and cut Wingate off.

His heart rose into his throat when he saw a column of cavalry ahead. Captain Hawkins's brass and gold braid gleamed in the Oklahoma sun. Slocum tried to get off the road and avoid the column, but Hawkins has seen him. The bugler tooted a warning note and the officer waved. Slocum didn't dare ride on without arousing suspicion. Explaining how he happened to be on the trail of the outlaw who had just robbed the Broken Arrow bank would be too complicated.

"Slocum," bellowed the officer. "I want a word with you."

He saw no way of avoiding the delay. Slocum mentally pictured Pisser Wingate riding down on Grace and shooting her before he found out she was a woman. He shuddered in spite of the day's rising heat when he thought what the bounty hunter might do if he *did* know she was a woman. Memories of Brighton and Dantley refused to die.

"Howdy, Captain," he said, trying to look unconcerned. Slocum didn't think he was doing a good job. The officer eyed him oddly.

"We found a fresh grave with our escaped prisoner in it. Signs pointed to quite a fight in the camp, too. Blood enough for a dozen men to have been cut down showed that."

"Do tell."

"What do you know of it?"

"Can't rightly say I know anything. I did speak with Dantley. That was before he got out of your lockup. I had nothing to do with helping him escape."

"I checked on that possibility," Hawkins said, eyes still narrowed and suspicious. "You come out clean enough on that score. You're in this up to your earlobes, though. There have been more bank robberies since you and that damned wagon train showed up in these parts than in the past year."

"I haven't robbed any banks. Neither has Jethro August."

"We're still checking down Texas way to see about him. I don't know where to look to find out about you."

Slocum chafed at the delay. Wingate was riding a slower horse than Grace, but he had a lead—and he was a skilled tracker. Grace didn't have time to lay a false trail that would fool the bounty hunter.

"I don't take kindly to crime, Slocum."

"You asking me to keep on riding?"

"I want to know where you were going in such an all-fired hurry." Hawkins pinned him with his icy stare. Slocum felt like a sick animal being studied by a vet.

"Away from here," Slocum said, knowing he had lost any hope of overtaking Wingate. What the bounty hunter might do to Grace only fueled the need for revenge that blazed higher and higher inside him. Wingate wouldn't let the preacher's daughter live.

"We're hunting for the bounty hunter, Wingate, too," said Captain Hawkins. "We've got some serious questions to ask him about Dantley. Evidence shows he was there. Don't know anyone else around who makes that deep a track."

Hawkins paused for several seconds, then added, "We found the other two. Brighton and Villalobos. I've got some real *hard* questions to ask Wingate."

"Good luck in tracking him down, Captain. If there's anything else, just drop by the wagon train and ask for me." Slocum figured this would give him a few extra hours to get the hell out of Oklahoma Territory. He didn't want the U.S. Army hunting for him, but neither did he want to be detained by them.

Pisser Wingate was vicious and had a long memory, horse-kicked-head notwithstanding.

"You're hiding something, Slocum. It had better not be anything important. I take law enforcement seriously."

"I've noticed that, Captain." Slocum settled down and let the column ride on past. He let out all the pent-up breath in his lungs and slumped. He had little chance of stopping Wingate now. He could have told Captain Hawkins about the bounty hunter and his chase after the Broken Arrow bank robber, but to have done so would have meant Grace's secret getting out.

The notion of the lovely raven-tressed woman spending time in a federal penitentiary didn't set well with Slocum. All she had done was rob a few banks. He hadn't heard of her killing anyone during the robberies—especially any innocent bystander. Most of all, Slocum couldn't forget how she had spared his life. She had had the sawed-off shotgun leveled and hadn't pulled the double triggers.

Wingate was a murderous son of a bitch. The best Slocum could tell, Grace Mason was simply looking for the excitement afforded by occasional crime. He remembered how Mrs. Throckmorton had said she fed needy children on the wagon train. The money wasn't what drew Grace to a life of crime—it was the sheer sport of the holdup.

Slocum glanced over his shoulder. The line of troopers had vanished in the direction of Broken Arrow. He didn't have much time. When Captain Hawkins found that the bank had been robbed and the direction taken by the solitary robber, he'd be back along this road in a flash. Slocum had to be long gone by then or he'd never be able to talk his way out of the Fort Gibson calaboose.

Slocum put his heels into the sorrel's side and raced off. His keen eyes studied the side of the road. Even with such intense study of the terrain, he rode so fast he almost missed the tracks leading off into a wooded area. He reined back hard and skidded to a halt.

"That way, old girl. Let's find Wingate and make sure he's buried six feet under this time." The horse turned one large brown eye around to stare at him. If the sorrel had been human, he would have interpreted the look as skeptical, but he had no idea what emotions ran through the animal, if any.

The horse neighed and obediently started on the proper trail. Slocum found two tracks leading into a marshy area. In less than a hundred yards he completely lost the trail. He dismounted and studied the ground carefully. The soft, spongy soil refused to hold any tracks. He moved his scrutiny up to the branches of thorny bushes and tree limbs, hoping to find broken twigs or torn fabric.

If Grace and Wingate had passed by, they had drifted like ghosts. He found no trace of them.

Slocum stopped and strained his ears, trying to listen for sounds that might tell him Wingate had found Grace. No screams, no pounding of horses' hooves, nothing came to him. He even tried sucking in deep breaths in a vain attempt to sniff out the smelly bounty hunter.

He dared hope that Grace had outsmarted Wingate. She had shown her expertise before with fake trails. He hoped she had managed to again elude her pursuit.

Slocum knew, though, that Pisser Wingate wasn't going to stop. If he didn't find his prey on the trail, he'd return to the wagon train. Why he hadn't shown up during the past three days, Slocum couldn't guess.

"Broken Arrow," Slocum decided. "That's where Wingate was when the bank was robbed. Something led him there in the first place. He'll go back to find Mason."

The horse bobbed her head in agreement—or she might have been trying to pull free to eat some marsh grass. Slocum didn't give her time to sample the juicy grass. He climbed into the saddle and turned back toward the sleepy little town that had experienced so much in the past twenty-four hours. Broken Arrow hadn't seen as many settlers in one day as had come in Jethro August's wagon train. Then they had a bank robbery. Slocum wouldn't have doubted that it was the town's first.

Slocum took another few minutes to cut a wide swathe

through the marshlands in the hope of finding evidence of Grace's safe passage. He found nothing, not even a trace of the bounty hunter's chase.

He got to the road leading back to Broken Arrow and hesitated. To take it directly meant running the risk of again meeting Captain Hawkins and his troopers. To ride off the road through the countryside would slow him down considerably.

The need for a speedy return to the preacher's wagon caused him to throw caution to the winds and ride on the road. Luck held for him this time. The cavalry officer hadn't yet learned of the bank robbery. If he had, the road would have been filled with carbine-carrying soldiers all bent on making their commander look like a hero.

Slocum circled the town, eyes peeled for any sign of Wingate. He didn't hear any gunfire, which heartened him. Pisser Wingate would have sparked an all-out gunfight if anyone had seen him in the mood he was in. The bounty hunter was looking for his prey. He wouldn't let anyone stand in his way now.

He slid off his horse and hit the ground running when he got to Mason's wagon. Slocum flipped the leather thong off his Colt Navy's hammer and drew the precision-machined weapon. A quick look around failed to turn up Grace, her father—or Wingate.

"Who are you looking for, Mr. Slocum? That slut of a woman who disgraces her father's good name?"

Slocum spun, six-shooter leveled and ready. His sights centered on Mrs. Throckmorton's distended belly. The woman squeaked like a stepped-on mouse and put her hand to her lips.

"I . . . I'm sorry. I didn't mean that about Miss Mason. It's just that she . . . I mean all her carrying on with those other three men. And you. Not that I mean *you*—"

"Where are they?" Slocum demanded, cutting through the woman's nervous explanations. "Where's Mason?"

"I don't know how to apologize about saying that." The woman's round eyes fixed on the pistol still aimed at her.

Slocum let up on the hammer and lowered it. A quick motion put it into the soft leather cross-draw holster. "Don't bother apologizing," Slocum said coldly. "Have you seen Mason?"

"I . . . yes. He was spying on his daughter. I mean to say, he was sneaking a look under the canvas at her as she undressed! Imagine that! His very own daughter! He hurried off. I imagine to that worthless little frame building at the edge of town. Someone told me he was going to use it as a church, but no God-fearing preacher would watch his daughter like that."

Slocum didn't listen to the rest of Mrs. Throckmorton's denunciation of the preacher. He vaulted into the wagon and hunted through the chest holding Grace's clothing. He found the dusty red bandanna and the old canvas duster.

"Mr. Slocum, really!" the woman cried outside the wagon. "I never thought you were a sneak thief."

"Did Mason take anything with him into town? Did he look around inside here after Grace left?"

"Why, I do remember something of the sort. I couldn't see what it was he carried out. It must have been rather heavy from the way he cradled it."

The clothing Grace wore on her robberies was in the wagon. The old Remington wasn't.

Cole Mason had figured out who had committed the bank robberies—and he was carrying his old pistol.

"Which side of town?" he asked the flustered, nosy woman.

"That side. The far side. But really, Mr. Slocum. You

shouldn't be seen with the likes of Cole Mason. He was *watching* his own daughter disrobe."

Slocum left the woman muttering about rudeness and depravity. He rode like the wind to the other side of Broken Arrow. He couldn't find any deserted buildings. He jumped off and tethered his sorrel before going into a dry goods store.

"What can we do for you, mister?" asked the proprietor. The man's attitude was one of resignation.

"Where is Reverend Mason putting his church?"

"You're the second one to ask that," the clerk said, settling back down into a chair behind the counter.

"How long ago did the big, smelly man ask?"

"You friends with him?"

The dark expression on Slocum's face made the clerk blanch. "He didn't ask five minutes ago. I told him, just as I'm telling you, the new church is in the old undertaker's place. Clyde upped and moved into Fort Gibson last month. Left us in need of a new digger."

"An undertaker's parlor," Slocum said, astounded at the way fate moved. Before the day ended, Clyde would be sorry he had missed out on the business that had arrived on his old doorstep.

Slocum swung out onto the plank porch and fixed a look up the street on the undertaker's office. Part of the sign had been pulled down, but the exterior still carried its air of death.

Slocum considered getting his Winchester from his saddle and decided against it. Any gunfighting he did would be up close enough to be sure he ventilated Wingate's worthless hide. He had missed killing the bounty hunter too many times before. This time he would make damned sure he killed him.

A woman's scream came from the back room of the

undertaker's parlor. Slocum peered in a dirty window and saw only the sitting room for mourners. He kicked in the door and waited, six-shooter in his rock-steady hand.

"Don't," he heard Grace's voice from the back room. She screamed louder this time.

Slocum wanted to bull through the door into the back of the mortuary. Good sense held him back. Wingate might be using Grace to decoy him into a trap.

Moving cautiously, he peered through a hanging dark velvet drape. The dimly lit back room carried an eerie aspect to it. Shadows moved across other shadows, confusing the eye and refusing to give Slocum a clear target.

He slipped through the doorway and pressed his back against the wall as his eyes adjusted to the faint light. Grace cried out in pain again. Slocum swung to his left and homed in on a large, dark mass moving at the side of the room.

"Where is Deutsch?" came Wingate's gruff voice. "I tracked him down, and now he's gonna pay the price for his crimes."

"You're hurting me."

"I'll bust your goddamn arm off if you don't tell me where William Deutsch is."

Slocum tried to separate one phantom figure from the other. He didn't want to shoot blindly. He could kill Grace accidentally. Even worse, he didn't want to warn Wingate. If he lost the element of surprise, both he *and* Grace might end up dead.

He might not get more than one shot. Slocum wasn't superstitious, but Pisser Wingate was like some elemental force of nature. A ghost—or more. Slocum didn't cotton much to the supernatural, but he had seen the man endure too much not to believe just a mite.

"What do you want my papa for?" asked Grace.

Slocum admired her courage. He remembered then that she had thought Wingate was dead—that she had gunned him down in the clearing after he had tortured Dantley. How she managed to even speak without stammering after finding that the bounty hunter was still alive increased Slocum's opinion of her.

She was one hell of a spunky woman.

"He's William Deutsch. He killed my brother. He ruined my reputation. He's got a damned big reward on his head—or he did."

"He did?" she asked, startled. "What did he do?"

"He robs banks."

Grace laughed, in spite of Wingate's intimidating presence. "You're wrong. Papa is a preacher."

"He robbed banks fifteen years back, but he wormed out of those warrants. I don't know how he done it, but he did. But that don't matter none. I got him dead to rights. He's been robbin' banks from here all the way back to Arkansas."

"Papa? He's the most law-abiding man I know."

"You're his daughter," Wingate said. Slocum moved as softly as he could, trying to find a window to silhouette the bounty hunter. One good view and he could gun him down. Until then, he had to be more careful than he'd ever been.

"Papa would never do that."

"He did. I can't take him in for the old robberies, but the new ones I can. Him and those three what was with the wagon train did the crimes. They confessed."

"You tortured them," Grace snapped. Slocum saw the woman try to jerk free. Getting away from Pisser Wingate's grip was like trying to pull out of quicksand. "You killed Dantley as sure as if you had cut his throat. From what Captain Hawkins said earlier today, you skinned Brighton and stabbed Villalobos."

"I used this on them!"

Slocum saw the bright flash of the bowie knife in the air. He tried to follow the man's arm down and get a target. He couldn't. The back room of the undertaker's parlor was just too dark. Slocum kept moving, angling for a clean shot at the bounty hunter.

Grace screamed and fought, making it impossible for Slocum to get off a shot.

"I know what you did. I know because *I* robbed those banks. Dantley and Brighton and Villalobos and I robbed them all. Papa had nothing to do with it."

"You're a damned liar, woman." Wingate backhanded her. Slocum heard Grace gasp, then spit. He couldn't wait any longer. He had to stop Wingate.

"I am not!" Grace shouted. "I robbed the banks."

Before Wingate responded, the back door slammed open. Standing outlined in it was Cole Mason.

"Leave her be, Wingate. Your fight's with me."

"Deutsch!"

"You know me by that name. I'm William Deutsch. And I robbed the banks between here and Arkansas."

"Papa, no, I did it."

"Hush."

Slocum heard Grace grunt. He saw the thick shadows move and separate. One lay on the floor; Wingate had knocked the woman down. The huge one remaining had to be the bounty hunter.

Slocum cocked his Colt Navy just as Cole Mason pulled back his jacket and reached for the Remington stuck into his belt.

Pisser Wingate roared and threw his bowie knife. The heavy-bladed knife crunched into the door frame beside the preacher's head. Mason dragged out his six-shooter and lifted it.

A brilliant tongue of flame lashed forth from the dark form that was Pisser Wingate.

"Got you, you bastard!" the bounty hunter crowed.

Mason staggered, holding his belly. Slocum saw the dark outline of the Remington coming up. The black-powder pistol fired, filling the air with acrid, choking smoke. The slug went high and sang off a beam in the roof.

Wingate cackled like a crazy man. He did a small war dance and whooped in glee.

"Papa!" cried Grace. She forced herself to a sitting position and saw that her father lay dead in the doorway.

"Finished him off, the back-shooting son of a bitch. Now it's time to enjoy myself," said Wingate.

The huge bounty hunter turned from the fallen preacher. As he did, his bulk was outlined by the bright light from outside.

Slocum stepped up, aimed his Colt, and fired methodically. The first slug might have ended Wingate's life, but Slocum didn't stop. At measured intervals, he pumped one piece of hot lead after another into the bounty hunter's quivering body. After the fourth shot, Wingate lay unmoving on the floor beside Cole Mason.

Slocum emptied his six-shooter, just in case.

This time Pisser Wingate was very, very dead.

18

"He's dead," Grace Mason sobbed. "He's dead!"

Slocum put his arm around the woman's quaking shoulders. He didn't know how to quiet her.

"He died protecting you," he told her. "Wingate wasn't likely to give up when he didn't find the money."

"He would have," Grace said, trying to control the shudders wracking her body. She sniffed loudly and pulled free. She sat with her back against the wall. "Most of the money I took is hidden in the wagon. Where could I spend it?"

"There were places along the trail," Slocum said.

"Not really. I gave some to others on the wagon train. That's all. Dantley and the others spent their money. That's why they were caught." She smiled weakly. "Arlo was in love with me. But he never understood I only planned the robberies for the fun of it. I didn't need the money. Papa had plenty."

"A preacher?"

"I never asked. I just assumed he was frugal—and he was. He was tighter with a penny than any man I ever saw." Her eyes drifted to the body of her fallen father. "I loved him so much."

"You never knew he was a bank robber?"

"I never even suspected. When I found the old Remington it was like a revelation to me. I never thought he *used* it. I . . . I don't know what I thought. It just never seemed such a gentle, *boring* man could have been a robber."

Boring? Slocum snorted in contempt. Cole Mason—he refused to think of him as William Deutsch—had been anything but boring. The man had been a hellfire and brimstone preacher and had proven that his love for his daughter transcended any fear of death. He had died to save Grace.

"There're going to be questions from the authorities," he told her gently. "Can you answer them?"

"You're asking me to confess?" Her bright blue eyes turned round in astonishment.

"No!" He spoke more sharply than he'd intended. She jumped and huddled into herself, arms circling her body. He went to sit beside her. She didn't move away any farther.

"What I mean is that Captain Hawkins is going to want to know what happened. Are you able to blame everything on your father?"

"But he didn't do anything!" she protested.

"He's dead," Slocum said brutally. "Don't let his sacrifice go for naught. He saved you from Wingate. He can save you from the law, too."

"I truly thought Wingate was dead. I shot him. How did he come back like that?"

"I was watching," Slocum said. "And you didn't shoot him—I did." He cut off her protests. "You missed him by a mile. I fired just as you did and hit him in the head, but he was a tough one." Slocum glanced at the bounty hunter's body, just to be sure. Pisser Wingate lay unmoving. This time he was *dead*.

"I have to blame Papa for everything?"

"If they want to charge you for a crime, he did it," Slocum said. "He wouldn't object if he were still alive."

"No, he was a giving man. Not necessarily forgiving," she said. "But I must have been wrong. How did he find out?"

"Mrs. Throckmorton said he saw you changing from the duster and bandanna after you got back from the Broken Arrow robbery this morning."

"He was supposed to be here cleaning up the place. If only he hadn't died thinking I was a thief."

"You are."

Grace smiled strangely. A light came to her face unlike any Slocum had seen before. "Yes, I am. John, it feels wonderful to rob a bank. There is a thrill to planning it, then *doing* it. When I walk in, that big old shotgun leveled, there's respect and fear on their faces. I don't care about the money. It's the most wonderful feeling in the whole world!"

"I prefer the money to the danger," Slocum said.

Grace turned and looked at him squarely. "You've robbed banks, haven't you?"

"Let's see to your father," he said.

"I wish they hadn't buried him alongside Papa." Grace stared down at the twin mounds of dirt in the small cemetery.

"Wingate doesn't deserve anything more than being left in the sun for the buzzards," Slocum said. He had no good feelings toward the bounty hunter.

He looked up from the graves to the edge of the cemetery where Captain Hawkins waited with several of his soldiers. They leaned on their rifles, idly waiting for the mourners to leave the cemetery. There had been a few from the wagon train, including Jethro August, who had come to pay their last respects to Cole Mason.

Most of those Mason had traveled with for so long hadn't bothered to come.

"Ready?" Slocum asked.

Grace nodded. She pulled the black shawl around her shoulders. The hot sun beat down on them as they walked slowly toward the cavalry officer.

"Miss Mason," Hawkins said, touching the brim of his hat. "Sorry your pa died like this. I hate to trouble you at a time like this, but I need to ask some questions."

"Please, Captain Hawkins, make it fast. I just don't feel up to a lengthy questioning."

"Nothing like that, Miss Mason." Hawkins stared boldly at Slocum, as if wondering what the relationship between the preacher's bereaved daughter and the rootless drifter could be. "I need to know something about this bounty hunter."

"Wingate?"

"I have reason to believe he was behind the rash of bank robberies in the territory."

"What?" Grace stopped and stared, openmouthed.

"How did your father come to confront him?"

"Wingate is connected to the robberies?"

"We found evidence in his camp that he committed the Tahlequah and Fort Gibson robberies. Slips of paper, some money, items that were taken from customers in both banks. But that's not what I need to know."

"Captain Hawkins, the Reverend Mason knew of Wingate's crimes," Slocum said. "He tried to help the man."

"You mean Mason tried to talk him into confessing?"

"Into turning himself in," said Slocum. He elbowed Grace to keep her quiet. She tried to protest. "You know

Mason's past. He was a robber himself before he accepted his calling to the ministry."

"Wingate made a point of showing around an old wanted poster," Hawkins agreed. "We even had an old poster in the files. At least the adjutant remembers one, but it's disappeared."

"Mason knew firsthand the horror of being a law-breaker," Slocum said. "He had reformed and wanted others to accept their own responsibility and pay their debt to society."

"This doesn't . . ." Hawkins shook his head.

"What do you mean you found items from the robberies at Wingate's camp?" Grace asked.

"Just that. We thought he was nothing more than a bounty hunter out to collect a reward. It was a good cover for robbing the banks. Who'd ever think the man hunting the robber was doing the crime himself?"

They talked for several more minutes. Captain Hawkins ended by saying, "We'll need to talk further. I have a pay-roll to look after. Neither of you are planning to leave Broken Arrow, are you?"

"We've decided to settle here," said Slocum before Grace could speak. She nodded in mute agreement.

"Good. Best to you, and once more, Miss Mason, my condolences. Your father might be due a reward for stopping Wingate. We'll talk about that later, too."

When the cavalry officer rode off, Grace spun and demanded, "What's this about *Wingate* doing the robberies?"

"I found the money bags and other items in your wagon. I salted Wingate's camp with them."

"That's rich!" laughed Grace. "He spent his life tracking down my papa for bank robbery and Wingate ended up being accused of crimes *I* committed."

Slocum didn't mention the depth of Wingate's anger

over his brother and how he had lost his job.

"What now?" she asked.

Slocum looked toward the west. "I lied to Hawkins about settling down in Broken Arrow. If he'd thought I was going to ride on, he'd've put me in the Fort Gibson lockup until he was satisfied about Wingate."

"Well," Grace said, "I'm not going to let you."

"What?" Slocum was taken aback.

"I'm not going to let you leave me in this one-horse town."

"You'd come with me?"

"If you ask."

Slocum thought about it for several seconds, then smiled slowly. "Our paths will part sooner or later. But if you're willing, we might have some interesting times together."

Grace laughed and threw back her head, letting her long, dark hair float on the soft spring breeze. "What was that Captain Hawkins said about a payroll?"

"You'd rob the cavalry of its payroll? Hawkins wouldn't ever stop until he caught us."

"With the money, we could run fast and go far. John, think of the fun!"

"I'm thinking of the money," he admitted.

"We could make quite a team," Grace Mason said.

"Let's find out," Slocum said, meaning it. No matter where they went or how long they rode together, he knew it would never be dull.

And it wasn't.

SONS OF TEXAS

Book one in the exciting new saga of America's Lone Star state!

TOM EARLY

Texas, 1816. A golden land of opportunity for anyone who dared to stake a claim in its destiny...and its dangers...

Filled with action, adventure, drama and romance, *Sons of Texas* is the magnificent epic story of America in the making...the people, places, and passions that made our country great.

Look for each new book in the series!

JAKE LOGAN

___	0-425-09088-4	THE BLACKMAIL EXPRESS	$2.50
___	0-425-09111-2	SLOCUM AND THE SILVER RANCH FIGHT	$2.50
___	0-425-09299-2	SLOCUM AND THE LONG WAGON TRAIN	$2.50
___	0-425-09567-3	SLOCUM AND THE ARIZONA COWBOYS	$2.75
___	0-425-09647-5	SIXGUN CEMETERY	$2.75
___	0-425-09783-8	SLOCUM AND THE WILD STALLION CHASE	$2.75
___	0-425-10116-9	SLOCUM AND THE LAREDO SHOWDOWN	$2.75
___	0-425-10419-2	SLOCUM AND THE CHEROKEE MANHUNT	$2.75
___	0-425-10347-1	SIXGUNS AT SILVERADO	$2.75
___	0-425-10555-5	SLOCUM AND THE BLOOD RAGE	$2.75
___	0-425-10635-7	SLOCUM AND THE CRACKER CREEK KILLERS	$2.75
___	0-425-10701-9	SLOCUM AND THE RED RIVER RENEGADES	$2.75
___	0-425-10758-2	SLOCUM AND THE GUNFIGHTER'S GREED	$2.75
___	0-425-10850-3	SIXGUN LAW	$2.75
___	0-425-10889-9	SLOCUM AND THE ARIZONA KIDNAPPERS	$2.95
___	0-425-10935-6	SLOCUM AND THE HANGING TREE	$2.95
___	0-425-10984-4	SLOCUM AND THE ABILENE SWINDLE	$2.95
___	0-425-11233-0	BLOOD AT THE CROSSING	$2.95
___	0-425-11056-7	SLOCUM AND THE BUFFALO HUNTERS	$2.95
___	0-425-11194-6	SLOCUM AND THE PREACHER'S DAUGHTER	$2.95
___	0-425-11265-9	SLOCUM AND THE GUNFIGHTER'S RETURN (On sale December '88)	$2.95
___	0-425-11314-0	THE RAWHIDE BREED (On sale January '89)	$2.95

Please send the titles I've checked above. Mail orders to:

BERKLEY PUBLISHING GROUP
390 Murray Hill Pkwy., Dept. B
East Rutherford, NJ 07073

NAME_____

ADDRESS_____

CITY_____

STATE_____ ZIP_____

Please allow 6 weeks for delivery.
Prices are subject to change without notice.

POSTAGE & HANDLING:
$1.00 for one book, $.25 for each additional. Do not exceed $3.50.

BOOK TOTAL	$_____
SHIPPING & HANDLING	$_____
APPLICABLE SALES TAX (CA, NJ, NY, PA)	$_____
TOTAL AMOUNT DUE	$_____

PAYABLE IN US FUNDS.
(No cash orders accepted.)